# synopsis

Beckett Gray is a broken man. He's been going through the motions of life ever since his husband was taken from him five years ago. He doesn't believe in the supernatural, but when strange things begin to happen in his home, he's forced to admit something paranormal may be going on.

Karson Raycroft left this realm before his time because of a hit-and-run driver. Is he now reaching out to his husband, encouraging Beck to find love again and move on with his life?

On the verge of losing what little is left of his sanity, Beck hires medium Travis Watson to rid his home of whatever (or whoever) is causing the disturbances. But Travis may have his own demons that need exorcising before he can help Beck. Can Kar convince Beck and Travis that new love is possible together?

*Footprints on My Heart is a contemporary ghost story about two older guys finding love after tragedy, thanks to a matchmaking spirit.*

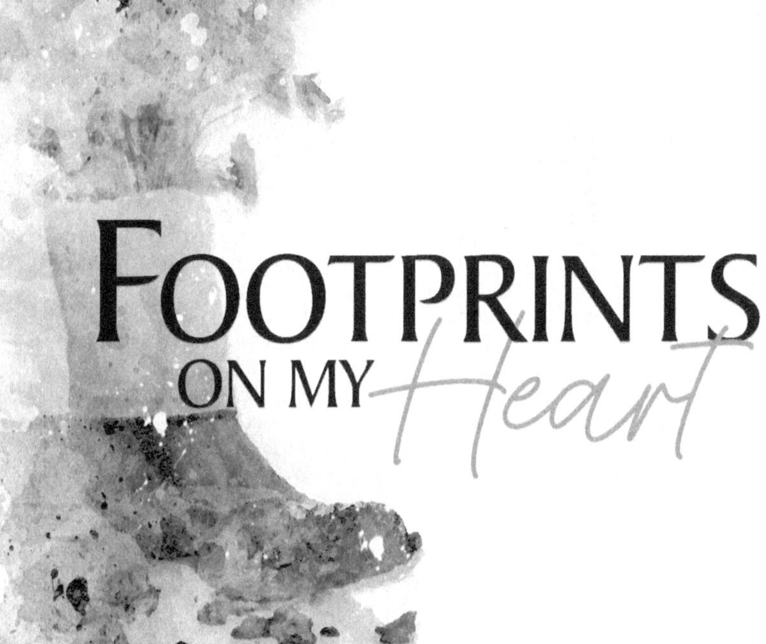

# FOOTPRINTS ON MY *Heart*

## RJ PETERSON

# author's note

In August 2024, I attended a virtual Writing Retreat.
Over the course of the 2-day event, we were provided with
several writing prompts.

One particular prompt inspired me to write this story:

***You find strange, muddy footprints
leading up to your front door.***

I hope you enjoying reading at as much as I did writing it.

# acknowledgments

As always, this book is very much a group effort...

David, my husband, friend, and travel partner. Thanks for your support and for making me laugh for 45+ years. Here's to new adventures and many more laughs!

My alpha/beta readers, Karen & Mia, my editor Dianne and proofreader Lisa – my books are *always* better thanks to your guidance and input. I couldn't have done it without each of you. And special thanks to Mia for suggesting the bonus chapter – Joseph deserved that!

Sharon, Melissa, Teresa, Tal, Hank, Meredith, Annabella, Ann, Sammi, Greg, and so many more—I can't imagine my life without you all—thanks for everything.

You all mean the world to me. Thank you!

*To the members of the*
*Working Draft Writing Retreat*

———

*Thanks for reacting as you did to the opening scene*
*and giving me the encouragement to tell*
*Beck, Travis, & Kar's story.*

*"Every love story is a ghost story."*

–David Foster Wallace

**Footprints on My Heart**

Copyright © 2025 by R.J. Peterson

All rights reserved.

No part of this book may be reproduced in any form or by any electronic or mechanical means, including information storage and retrieval systems, without written permission from the author, except for the use of brief quotations in a book review.

Cover design & interior design and formatting by Ron Perry Graphic Design, rperrydesign.com

Cover content is for illustrative purposes only.

Editing by Lyrical Lines, lyricallines.net

Proofreading by Lisa Lakeland, LesCourt Author Services, lescourtauthorservices.com

Digital ISBN: 978-1-967317-08-0

Print ISBN: 978-1-967317-09-7

This is a work of fiction. Names, characters, places and incidents are either used fictitiously or are the product of the author's imagination. Any resemblance to actual persons, living or dead, business establishments, events, or locales is entirely coincidental.

Any errors herein are mine and mine alone.

All products and/or brand names mentioned are registered trademarks of their respective holders/companies.

**This novel contains mature sexual content. Reader discretion is advised.**

## No Generative AI Training Use.

For avoidance of doubt, Author reserves the rights, and does not grant permission to any individual/company/publisher/platform any rights to reproduce and/or otherwise use the Work in any manner for purposes of training artificial intelligence technologies to generate text, including without limitation, technologies that are capable of generating works in the same style or genre as the Work, unless said individual/company/publisher/platform obtains Author's specific and express permission to do so. Nor does any individual/company/publisher/platform have the right to sublicense others to reproduce and/or otherwise use the Work in any manner for purposes of training artificial intelligence technologies to generate text without Author's specific and express permission.

In addition, no artificial intelligence (A.I.), predictive language software, or generative design software was used in any part of the creation of this book or its cover, nor will it ever be for any of my works.

<h1>one</h1>

BECKETT

*ALL I WANT IS a glass of bourbon and to relax in my recliner.*

It had been a long day at work, and I was happy to finally be pulling into the driveway of my modest Craftsman-style home. I'd forgotten to stop and take the day's mail out of the box at the curb, so I trudged back down the driveway, silently reprimanding myself for my thoughtlessness. *I must be even more tired than I imagined.*

As I approached the front porch, I noticed some mud on the steps. It had rained earlier in the day—a steady downpour for most of the morning—but the sun had been out for a good part of the afternoon. *Hmmm, did someone stop by?*

The mud turned into more clearly defined footprints as I walked toward the front door. "Well, that's odd," I said aloud to no one in particular. "The prints lead up to the door, but they don't appear to turn around and leave."

My mind was too cloudy to make complete sense of it, so I

dismissed the thoughts and entered my home. Tossing my keys and the mail on the small table in the entry, I shrugged out of my coat and hung it on the coat-tree. I paused, detecting the faint odor of decaying leaves.

My gaze shifted downward, where I could make out faint footprints on the hardwood, left by what appeared to be muddy boots. The coarse tread pattern of the soles was somehow familiar, but how I knew this eluded me. I heard nothing in the house, and you know that feeling you get in your gut that tells you there's someone else home? I didn't feel that. No, my home felt empty.

Wait, something stirred in my gray matter. *Could it be? No, that's impossible.* I shook my head to banish those thoughts.

"Is anyone here?" I said out loud, trying to sound braver than I felt. I peered first into the living room, then across the hall into the dining room. Seeing no one, I tiptoed down the hall to the kitchen and den. Nothing. I retraced my steps and crept up the stairs as quietly as I could. After checking all the rooms and finding nothing, I felt foolish. Why on earth would I think there was actually someone in my house? I quickly changed into a T-shirt and some sweats and went back downstairs to pour myself that well-deserved bourbon.

As I placed the bottle back in the cupboard, I caught movement out of the corner of my eye. Turning to see if there was actually something there, I ...

———

MY EYES SLOWLY OPENED; disorientation rattled my brain. I was on the floor of my kitchen. Apparently, my stockinged feet had slipped as I turned, and I had tumbled down, hitting my head on the terrazzo floor.

I stood slowly, checking to make sure nothing was bruised or broken. Not even a significant bump on the back of my head, so that was a relief. Then my mind replayed what had happened.

Had I seen something? A shadow? A person? No, it couldn't be a person, could it? My thoughts wandered once again to the somehow-familiar tread pattern in the footprints. *But it couldn't possibly be...*

I lifted the crystal glass of amber liquid to my lips and sipped. It burned slightly as it slowly slid down my throat, settling into a warmth in my belly that calmed me. Thinking once again of the muddy footprints, I went back down the hall to the foyer. No footprints were visible on the hardwood. What the hell? Had I imagined it? Karson would never track mud in from the garden.

But wait, Kar was gone.

I took another sip and slowly walked into the den, shaking my head. Sitting in my recliner, I pondered everything that had happened since I got home. None of it made sense. *Perhaps I'm just going crazy.*

———

I ARRIVED at work the next day still feeling quite restless. The things I saw or thought I had seen the previous evening at home had made for an awful night's sleep. I woke often and had strange dreams of walking in the woods behind our home with Kar.

Donning my white jacket, I prepared for my day behind the pharmacy counter, where I supervised a handful of other pharmacists and pharmacy techs as we filled prescriptions and spoke with customers who had questions about the medications they took. My best friend, Valerie, worked beside me and immediately sensed something was amiss.

"Sleep on the wrong side of the bed last night, Beck?" she asked.

"I'm the only one who sleeps in that bed now, so aren't both sides mine? How would I know if one of them was wrong?" I answered, irritability coloring my words.

"Calm down, Beck. It's me you're talking to," Val chided.

"I'm sorry. Some weird shit went on when I got home yesterday, and I'm still out of sorts."

"What? Tell me what happened." Care was evident in her tone.

As best I could, I explained the footprints and seeing a shadow of something or someone, desperately trying not to sound completely unhinged.

"You're sure you're not concussed? Here, let me feel the back of your head." I waited patiently as Val probed my noggin, knowing that if I resisted it would only be worse. Val was like the older sister I never wanted. But I loved her dearly, so I put up with the endless advice and occasional mothering. "Okay, I don't feel anything," she concluded. "So what do you think it was? I know you're not gonna want to hear this, but you know it sounds like Kar."

"Val, you and I both know that he's gone," I whispered, trying to make it less real. In many ways, I still mourned for him. "Besides, you know I don't believe in that supernatural shit." Karson Raycroft was my dead husband, the victim of a hit-and-run five years earlier.

"Just because *you* don't believe doesn't mean it isn't real," Val said quietly as she lightly touched my shoulder.

Ignoring her comment, I glanced at the clock on the far wall. "We open in five minutes, people," I announced.

————

"C'MON, let's get a drink. My treat," Val said as we strode to our cars at the far end of the parking lot after work.

"I think I'll pass tonight, Val," I replied. Last night had really shaken me up, and I wasn't really in the mood to socialize although the thought of going home frightened me somewhat.

"Nonsense. I don't want you sitting in that empty house, thinking about last night," Val told me. "Besides, it's Friday, and we always go to Fiddler's for a drink. Now get your ass over there." She knew me too well. And she was right. Drinks and sometimes dinner on Friday nights at Fiddler's was a ritual for us, especially once Kar passed.

"Fine. I'll see you there." No sense in fighting her. If I went home, she'd just follow me there anyway.

We got seats at the bar almost immediately thanks to Dennis, who'd been pouring drinks for us for more years than I cared to count.

"Evening, guys," he said, placing drinks in front of us before we could even order. A cosmo for Val and bourbon on the rocks for me. Okay, so we were predictable but never boring. I did my best to be in the moment with Val even as I fretted about going back to my empty house alone.

# two

BECK

I entered my home cautiously. I sincerely didn't want a repeat of last night. Much to my relief, I saw no footprints on the porch, and upon entering the foyer, everything looked normal.

Val and I had ordered more food than we could possibly eat, so I took my leftovers into the kitchen and stuck the take-out box into the fridge. As I opened the door, I caught a whiff of something. It took my brain a few moments to identify it. It smelled like the fertilizer that had Kar used in the gardens. Odd. I had a black thumb, and after Kar's passing, I hired a landscaping company to mow the lawn and tend to the gardens. They weren't scheduled to come by until next week, and even so, they wouldn't have been in the kitchen, so where was the odor coming from?

I opened the back door and peered out. Nothing. I shut

and relocked the door, turning toward the kitchen island. Lying there were two black-eyed Susans, stems crossed.

"No!" I cried out, backing away from the island. I retreated to my bedroom, stripping quickly and diving under the covers like a man-child afraid of the dark. *What's happening to me? Those flowers—they were the same blooms used in the boutonnieres when Kar and I got married. Why are they in my kitchen?*

Sleep did not come easily that night.

———

I DRAGGED myself out of bed on Saturday morning, tired and irritable. When I entered the kitchen to make coffee, there were no flowers on the island. Had I imagined it all? Perhaps I really was going crazy.

After my third cup of coffee, I seriously contemplated calling Val. But I knew she'd just chalk this up to another example of some ghostly hogwash, and I really didn't want to hear that right now. We didn't keep secrets from each other, so I promised myself I'd tell her eventually. Right then, however, I needed time to process everything that was happening.

"Kar," I said aloud, "if this is really you, show me something that will help me believe."

Nothing. I waited a few moments, scanning the room for some sign. Still nothing. I ventured out to the hall and foyer, even opening the front door to peer at the porch floor. More nothing.

See? In my mind, this was proof that all that talk of paranormal activity and psychic phenomena was just horseshit. If Kar were really here, he would have responded to my plea, right?

Satisfied that I'd proven or disproven—depending on your point of view—that none of this was real, I cleaned up my breakfast dishes and perused the contents of my fridge and pantry. After all, today was grocery day.

———

The rest of my day passed normally. I shopped for food and a few other items, then put everything away once I returned home. I dutifully checked the foyer and hall again, as well as the kitchen, but saw no evidence of Kar or any other suspicious activity for that matter. I spent the rest of the afternoon in the den, working on my writing. Before Kar passed, I'd started it as a hobby in my spare time. I'd dabbled with writing throughout my life, but Kar had encouraged me to do more. I'd had a few short stories accepted and published in a local magazine and was now trying my hand at something longer.

Just before five, my phone rang.

"Hey, Val." We sometimes got together on Saturday nights to watch a movie or play cards—either cribbage or Five Crowns —and I was sure that's why she was calling. I know, we lead such exciting lives.

"How's it going, Beck? Get your grocery shopping done?" See, no secrets between us.

"Yes, Mom," I teased. "Everything's put away just like you taught me."

"Don't be an ass," she said. "So are we getting together tonight?"

"Um, I'd rather not," I begged off. "I'm still a bit unsettled because of the muddy footprints the other night." While that was certainly part of it, I was also afraid I'd say something about the flowers and really wasn't in the mood for another lecture about the unknown. "I'll probably just read for a while and make it an early night."

"Okay." Val sounded disappointed. "I guess I can wait a week before I kick your ass in cards again."

"In your dreams," I returned. "I'll mop the floor with your scrawny butt, and you know it!"

"Just take care of yourself, sweetie," Val told me. "And if anything else happens, let me know. I want to help."

I choked a bit at her sincerity. I really did hate deceiving her, but it was for the best. "Thanks, Val. I appreciate it."

We rang off, and I went to reheat my leftovers for a solitary dinner.

———

MONDAY MORNING DAWNED bright and quite warm. I showered and dressed, feeling lighter than I had in a few days.

No other unusual activities had manifested over the weekend. Well, except for that one little thing that I wasn't even sure was all that unusual. It might have just been me.

On Sunday afternoon, I had been rummaging through the drawers in my desk, looking for a bill that I thought for sure had arrived in the mail earlier in the week. I didn't find it. Later, I walked by the desk and saw something unexpected on the blotter. Kar's driver's license.

After he died, I'd put it, along with a few other things he kept in his wallet, in the top left drawer of the desk. It felt right having part of him close to me there, and I'd occasionally flip through the items—license, insurance card, photo of us taken at our wedding, a now-expired credit card—looking at them somehow gave me comfort shortly after his passing.

I distinctly remembered seeing the license yesterday but

didn't remember taking it out of the drawer. But maybe I had. I just wasn't completely sure at this point. But I quickly talked myself out of thinking it was the sign I'd asked for. No, I'd just removed it from the drawer without realizing it and neglected to put it away. That was my story, and I was sticking to it.

I parked in my usual spot, and Val pulled in next to me before I had a chance to get out of my vehicle.

"Good morning, sunshine!" she said in greeting.

"Hey, Val!" I said happily.

"How was the rest of your weekend?"

"Good," I replied. "No more weirdness going on. I paid some bills and got some reading done."

She looked at me a bit strangely as if she somehow knew I was lying, but she didn't say anything. As long as there was no real evidence to the contrary, I could keep believing I was just imagining things. Grief was like that sometimes, right?

# three

KARSON

*Oh, my sweet Beck, why can't you accept that I'm here? Why is it so hard for you to believe in an afterlife?*

I'd been wandering the interim plane for almost five years, trying to figure out a way to convince Beck that he could find love again while still keeping part of me in his heart. He wasn't really living anymore; he was merely existing—broken in so many ways. Oh, sure, he played a good game, convincing himself that everything was okay, but I knew he was slowly dying inside. In fact, if it weren't for Val, I was sure he would have already died of loneliness and joined me here.

What folks don't understand is that when someone dies, you don't automatically understand everything that's happening to you. It's all very disconcerting, and despite what some books or movies have tried to insinuate, there's no secret guidebook or way station that tells you everything you need to know.

I remember that day almost five years ago as if it were yesterday. Well, time moves a bit differently here, so it may well have been yesterday in the whole scheme of things. Anyway, I remember spending part of the day in the garden. In life, I worked as an editor for academic publications—mostly textbooks and the occasional article for a magazine or journal. For a few years I'd tried teaching at the college level but much preferred the solitary work of an editor. I worked from home and made my own hours, which suited me and my life with Beck just fine.

It had been a typical day. A bit of editing in the morning, followed by a few hours in the garden, which I loved. Weeding, planting, pruning, I loved it all. I had spent a fair amount of time in the front garden that day, leaving my muddy boots— which Beck absolutely hated for some reason—on the front porch with a small bouquet of wildflowers sticking out of the top of one of them.

I went upstairs and changed into my running clothes, then set out on a run through the neighborhood. The area where we lived was rather secluded, with houses spread pretty far apart, but I never encountered any issues jogging the streets there.

Until that day.

I'd been out for nearly an hour and was almost home. I was thinking about dinner that night. Pasta with chicken and vegetables in a light wine-and-cream sauce. It was one of Beck's favorites. Suddenly, I was struck from behind. Boom! Instant pain, then just as quickly, nothing. Before I knew it, I was standing next to my body. Well, that's how it felt. I wasn't really corporeal anymore, but the sensation was that of looking down at my now-dead body. The car that hit me never stopped. I tried to shout at them, but they couldn't hear me since I was no longer among the living. I caught part of their license plate

—D75S—not that it would do any good. After all, whom could I tell?

A few minutes later, a car slowed as it drove by my body. The driver pulled over but didn't get out of their vehicle. I assumed they called 911 since an ambulance and police car showed up several minutes later.

At some point as all of this was happening, I realized that I was indeed dead. It was a sobering thought, and I leaned against a nearby tree. *Shit, what do I do now?* I'm not sure why, but I had an overwhelming feeling that I should be home. So I began walking. Again, I didn't actually have a body, but my brain—or whatever the dead equivalent of that is—was still processing everything as if I had an actual mind and body. Rather than question it, I simply accepted it as the way it was.

———

SHORTLY AFTER I walked up our driveway and sat on the steps leading to the front porch, I saw a police car pull up. I was pretty sure these were the officers from the scene of my accident, but frankly, I hadn't been paying that much attention to what they looked like, just having realized I was dead and all.

They approached the front door, walking right past me. When there was no answer, they returned to their patrol car and waited. Soon, Beck turned into the driveway in our Kia Sportage.

As the three of them approached the steps, I heard one of the officers say, "Perhaps we should go inside."

And Beck shouted, "Just tell me." They told him I was dead, and he collapsed.

I sat next to his unconscious body on the porch, my non-body sobbing uncontrollably. I did not want him to have to deal with my death. Once I got control of myself and knew that Beck was awake again, I walked away. I couldn't be there, watching him mourn. Call me a coward, but I just felt so helpless that it tore me apart. I didn't go very far. As the days passed, I checked on Beck now and then. But it was too painful to stay close for long. At least in the beginning.

———

LIKE I SAID, I wandered around. I felt ... a bit of a pull, I guess you'd call it. The feeling that I should head in a certain direction. In my case, it was east. But I ignored it, not ready to leave Beck just yet. Part of me wanted, or needed, to make sure he was okay.

As I said earlier, there's no handbook to tell you everything you need to know, but after a few days, I found another soul such as myself—I knew they were deceased, as they lacked most of their color and were semitransparent—also meandering along with no apparent purpose.

"Hello," I said tentatively, unsure as to the etiquette of speaking with other "spirits" as I'd come to think of myself.

"Hi," she said quietly.

"My name is Karson. Have you been here long?"

"I'm Sarah," she replied. "I think it's been about two years since I got here. At first I wasn't really sure what was happening, so I haven't been very good at keeping track of time."

"I've only been here a few days," I told her. "Are there others like us?"

"Yes, I've met several of us here. But be careful. Some are nice while others are deceitful. Not everything you hear from other spirits will be true."

"Thank you for telling me. I've been feeling like I should go east, but I don't think I'm ready yet," I said. "Have you felt like that too?"

"I did at first. That's the pull to fully cross over to the next plane," Sarah said. "But I'm not ready yet either. I haven't found out what it is yet, but I think there's something I need to do before I can move on."

"That's good to know. I appreciate the fact that you're willing to share."

"Oh," she said suddenly. "I have to go!"

And with that, she hurried off. I looked around quickly, wondering if Sarah had seen something that scared her off, but I found nothing amiss. Ah, well, it seemed there was a lot of things I'd need to get used to in this new level of existence.

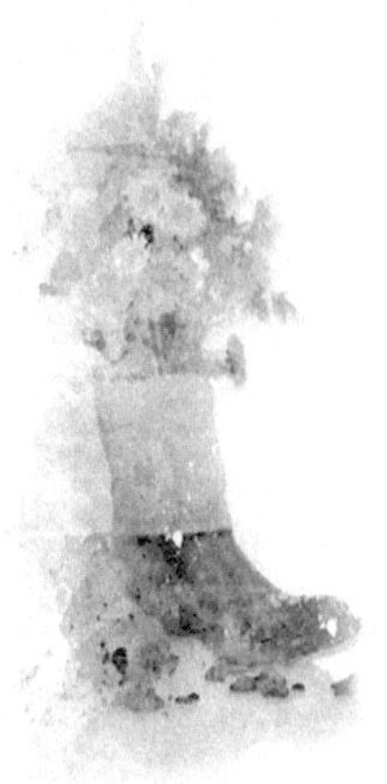

# four

TRAVIS

THE SHRILL RING of the phone woke me. The clock on the nightstand read seven thirty-five. I reached for the phone, nearly knocking over the almost-empty bottle of Jack Daniels.

"Travis Watson, Paranormal Investigations," I answered groggily. *Why on earth was someone calling at this ungodly hour?*

"I'm sorry to call so early, but I think my house is haunted." The frantic voice on the other end of the phone spoke rapidly. "Can you help me, *please*?"

I stifled a groan. The last thing I wanted to do right then was evaluate and possibly cleanse a house—especially the way my head was pounding—but hell, it *was* my job.

"Certainly, madam," I consented, trying to sound somewhat professional. "Give me your address, and I'll be there as soon as I can."

Groaning once again, I dragged my sorry ass out of bed and into the shower. Some days I hated my life.

———

Several hours later, I sat at a small coffee shop a few blocks from the house I'd received the call about. Indeed, the house had been haunted by a feisty but immature spirit. An adolescent that unfortunately had died too soon and ended up wandering the interim plane, unsure what they should do next. Often, when a younger person passes, a dead relative will come to the interim plane and help guide them along. But in this case, no one showed up, and the spirit was unsure of all that was happening. So the boy simply did what boys do to entertain themselves and found a home where they proceeded to create a little havoc for no other reason than they thought it was fun.

I did what needed to be done—basically talked to the boy, who called himself Charlie, and explained what was happening to him, urging him to move on to a better place. It took a bit of convincing, not to mention a psychic "push" or two so that he could see the way more clearly. The house was now free of his spirit—at least for the time being.

From the little I know about these things, some spirits either get lost on the way or are just a bit too stubborn and manage to return—although that was a rather rare occurrence. I'd explained to Mrs. Jackson that it was a possibility, and that if she noticed any unusual activity, she should call me, and I'd return to clean it up as well.

I was presently consuming large amounts of sugary pastries and caffeine. Psychic work takes a substantial amount of energy, and my resources get depleted rather quickly. If I'm lucky, I can find a ley line—sort of an energy conduit—in the area and tap into that, but these days, those are few and far between. Luckily, my cozy little home was situated just above one of the few such lines in the area, and a few hours of rest would refill my personal reservoirs to the max. But home was several miles away, so for now, I'd need to make do with the delicacies this shop had to offer.

I picked up my phone and transferred Mrs. Jackson's payment from PayPal to my bank account, finished my bear claw, and headed out the door.

———

IT WAS dark outside when I woke from my nap on the living room couch. I was feeling refreshed after today's exhausting work, especially for a hack like me.

Yeah, I said it—hack.

True, I am a medium, a sensitive, a psychic, a dispeller of spirits. I have the calling or the gift, whatever. I can chat with spirits—or ghosts if you prefer that term. I can sometimes discern something about someone—their past or future—but the reality is that I don't have much in the way of formal training for what I do. Mostly, I just muddle my way through things. Fortunately, my instincts are good, so I never get seriously hurt and manage to do some good along the way. And as far as I know, I am the only one like me in the area. At least the only one who really has the gift. As a result, I actually make a decent living doing what I do.

The phone on the end table rang. Unless it was a possible client, it could only be one person, my best friend—argh, who was I kidding, my only friend—Tony.

"Hi, Tony," I answered, seeing his face on the screen.

"Hello, mate. Whatcha up to this evening?" Tony's faint British accent still wrapped itself around his words even after living all these years in the States.

"I just woke up from a nap. So basically, no plans."

"A nap, eh? Does that mean you had a job today?" Tony Dawes owned the Raven's Claw, a holistic, new-age type shop in town. He stocked mostly books, along with an assortment of other magick items. You know, crystals, herbs, tarot decks, and the like. He knew me quite well.

"Yeah. Got a call first thing this morning, and I had to help a young spirit along the way. He'd been causing some mischief in someone's home."

"Ah. It sounds like you spent all your reserves in the process. Totally knackered out, eh?" Yeah, Tony knew me very well.

"You know me, Tone, I tend to leak out a bit of power when I work. But I'm feeling much better now."

"Mate, how long have I been telling you that I know someone who might be able to help you out with that? You gotta chat with Auntie Mae."

"I dunno, Tone. I've been muddling along fine so far—" I began.

"But it's not so fine on days like this, is it?" Tony cut me off.

When my grandmother saw that I had the gift, she tried to teach me how to use and control it. But I was young, a little arrogant, and didn't have time for such nonsense. I didn't pay much attention to what Gran was trying to tell me back then, and now she's gone.

They say hindsight is twenty-twenty, and yeah, I wish I'd paid more attention to what she had to say, but I can't now. And so I do my best with the little I know. I'm not exactly sure why I was so resistant to meeting Tony's Auntie Mae. Maybe I felt like it was cheating on Gran. Or maybe it's just that I was embarrassed that I didn't listen and learn when I had the chance.

"Okay," I told Tony. "I'll think about it."

"Good. Let me know when you're ready. Now, since you've got no plans for the evening, you wanna grab a bite to eat or summat?"

"No, I think I'll just lie low tonight, Tone. But I'll call you tomorrow. Maybe we can get together then."

# five

BECK

MY WEEK PASSED WITHOUT INCIDENT. Work was fairly quiet, all things considered. And no strange happenings at home, to the point I'd almost forgotten about the earlier occurrences. Until Saturday.

I'd woken up and gone down to the kitchen to have breakfast. All nice and normal. I needed to run a few errands but put that off until the afternoon and instead tidied up the den and kitchen a bit. I had a cleaning service come in every two weeks, but in between I did my best to keep the place from becoming too messy.

Around eleven, I walked down to the mailbox at the end of the driveway, taking the long route from the back door in the kitchen. Upon my return, I noticed something on the front porch. As I went up the steps, I saw traces of mud leading up to the old boots standing sentinel at the front door. In one of the boots was a small bouquet of wildflowers matching those growing along one side of the house. *Just like the day he was killed.*

I stood transfixed. Kar used to do this all the time. But he'd been gone for nearly five years, so how was this possible? I started to back away but quickly changed my mind. Instead, I snatched the bouquet and took it with me, quickly walking to the kitchen door.

The stems of the flowers appeared torn as if they'd been hastily ripped from the garden, so I trimmed them carefully, just as Kar had taught me so many years ago, and set them in a vase of water on the kitchen island. Was Val right? Had Kar returned from the grave to try and tell me something? I was so confused. Too shook up to do any shopping, I placed a quick grocery order for delivery and retreated to the den to try and figure it out.

I grabbed a notebook and pen, along with my iPad, and sat in my recliner, deep in thought. I made note of everything that had occurred, starting with the muddy footprints a week ago and ending with the bouquet in the boots this morning. Opening my tablet, I searched for stories about paranormal activity, trying to make sense of all that had happened.

After a few hours of research, I was as confused as ever and decided that I needed to discuss this all with Val. We were meeting for brunch in the morning, a monthly treat for us. I'd talk to her over mimosas and eggs Benedict.

---

"Good morning, sunshine!" she greeted me outside of the restaurant. Ugh. I hate morning people.

"Is it really?" I practically growled at her.

"Oh! Hangover, or just still in a bad mood, like you were on Friday?"

"I'm not hungover, but how can you be this cheerful so early in the morning?"

"Honey, it's almost ten thirty," she practically purred.

"Like I said, so early!" I realized how ridiculous I sounded and attempted a smile.

"So if you're not hungover, what's got your panties in such a bunch today?"

"Something else happened," I mumbled.

"Tell me, Beck. More footprints?"

"Well, actually, it's been a couple of things. Last Friday, it was black-eyed Susans on the kitchen island. Two of them just lying there. I saw them when I put away my leftovers."

"Shit! You had those at your wed—"

"Yeah, I know," I cut her off. "Why is this happening?"

"I don't know, Beck." She paused. "Wait. You said a couple of things. What else happened?"

"Yesterday morning, I went down the drive to fetch the mail, and when I walked back to the house, there were, um ..." My voice broke.

"Hey." Val covered my hand with hers. "Whatever it is, it's gonna be okay."

"There were more traces of mud on the front steps, and one of Kar's boots near the door had a bouquet of wildflowers in it." I was close to tears. "Shit, Val, I feel like I'm going crazy!"

"First of all, you are *not* going crazy." Val was adamant. "Folks going off the rails don't usually know that it's happening, so I'm pretty sure you're okay."

"Gee, that's reassuring," I deadpanned.

"Crap!" Val exclaimed. When she spoke next, her voice had

softened. "I just realized it's almost the anniversary of, you know, that night."

"Yeah, I thought of that yesterday," I admitted. Kar had been killed on the twenty-eighth of this month—September—five years ago. It was less than a month away.

"I think you need to consider that this may be a sign," she said quietly.

"You know I don't believe in that shit, Val. If Kar was gonna come back to haunt me or whatever it is that ghosts supposedly do, why didn't he do it sooner? Because all that spirit nonsense is just that—nonsense."

"I wish you wouldn't say things like that, Beck," she replied, sounding rather frustrated. "There are many of us who believe and have had experiences that convince us there are other realms where our loved ones go when they leave us."

"I'm sorry, Val. I know you believe in all of that, but my logical brain just has difficulty wrapping my head around things like ghosts and such." I hated to disappoint her, but that's the way I felt. "But I'll admit that I did try and do some research yesterday about all of this hocus-pocus, and frankly, it left me more confused than anything else."

"Just promise me that you'll think about it," Val pleaded. "I'm going to send you an article or two that I'd like you to read. Please, Beck. Do it for me. I think it could help you understand what's going on."

"Fine," I agreed. Maybe I'd been too dismissive of her beliefs. *Okay,* I told myself, *I'll read what she sends me.* But I was not convinced it would help.

———

WHEN I GOT HOME from brunch, I grabbed my iPad and sat in my favorite recliner, opening the email from Val containing not two but five links to online articles.

*Nothing like a little overkill, Val.* I smiled to myself, recalling our first meeting so many years ago at the Massachusetts College of Pharmacy.

*I was sitting at a table all to myself in the cafeteria during the first week of my first year, trying to make sense of the chemistry book I was reading while having lunch. Suddenly, this whirlwind of a person plunked a stack of books on the other side of the table, rapidly saying, "Is it okay if I sit here? Fine, thanks. Whew! I'm Valerie, by the way. Valerie Grimes. But you can call me Val."*

*I shook her outstretched hand. "Beckett Gray, but most people call me Beck." Her personality seemed larger than her five-five frame. She had short, spiky black hair with brilliant blue eyes that seemed to dance when she spoke.*

I snapped out of my reverie. Val's eyes still sparkled all these years later. Over time, she'd become more than a friend. She was family. Especially since Kar's passing. I couldn't imagine my life without her.

By the time I finished reading all the articles she'd sent, I began to think that perhaps I'd reacted too harshly to some of her opinions. I wasn't ready to admit that I suddenly believed in all of this supernatural stuff, but I was at least willing to do some additional research and maybe, just maybe, adjust my thinking.

A couple of the articles that she'd sent me had links to other stories, so I dove into them as well. I'd expected the stories to be dry and fact filled, attempting to validate the existence of the paranormal, and a couple were like that. But several were eyewitness accounts of such activity told by friends and loved ones who'd experienced it all firsthand. Those stories were fascinating, and many mimicked my own experience. I read long into the night.

# six

BECK

I WAS busy with paperwork when Val got to work on Monday morning. I may have arrived early for the very purpose of being busy when Val got there so that I could avoid discussing the articles she'd sent me. But she saw right through my ploy.

"Did you read any of the articles I sent you, Beck?" she asked pointedly.

"Yes," I sighed, removing my reading glasses and looking at her. "I read all of them and even did a little research of my own."

"Really?" Val asked. There was something akin to respect in her voice as if she hadn't thought I'd follow through. "And?"

"And what?" I said innocently.

"Don't play dumb with me, mister." *Damn, she caught me again!* "And what do you think? Did anything you read change your mind at all?"

"I must admit, I'm a bit more open to all of this than I was last week. But you need to give me some time, Val. I believed certain things for so long. It's gonna take a while for me to wrap my head around all this stuff."

"That's fine," she said, smiling warmly. "As long as you're willing to consider that there might be something to this, I'll give you time. But remember, I'm gonna keep working on you." She walked away.

———

THE REST of the day passed without incident. I think Val decided to let the matter lie for a while, giving me more time to consider the things I'd read.

Two nights later, I'd reread some of the notes I'd taken about paranormal activity and thought about the day Kar died.

I would never forget that night. It was nearly seven thirty, and the fading September light cast an orange-pink glow in the sky as I drove home. I remember passing an ambulance traveling in the other direction as I easily took the curve shortly before turning onto the street where Kar and I lived. I wasn't overly religious but said a short prayer for whoever required medical attention.

*I saw the police car in the driveway, and my heart sank.*

*"Beckett Gray?" one of the uniformed officers asked me.*

*"Yes. That's me."*

*"You live here with Karson Raycroft?" He checked his small black notebook.*

*"Yes. What is this about?"*

*"Perhaps we should go inside—" the other police officer began.*

*"Just tell me!" I demanded.*

*"Sir, there's been an accident. It appears that Mr. Raycroft was out jogging…"*

*"Yes, he does that almost every day. Some mornings and most evenings," I told them, my voice cracking. If I kept on talking, they wouldn't have the opportunity to tell me what I didn't want to hear.*

*"From what we can tell, it appears that Mr. Raycroft was struck from behind by a vehicle moving along Mill Road. The driver didn't stop. Some time later, another driver saw Mr. Raycroft on the ground and stopped to lend assistance. They called 911. I'm sorry to have to inform you that Mr. Raycroft didn't make it."*

*I came to later, lying on our front porch. One of the officers was kneeling beside me. "Mr. Gray. Beckett. Can you hear me?"*

*I had collapsed upon hearing the news about Kar.*

*"It can't be true," I wailed. "He can't be gone."*

*"I'm very sorry, Mr. Gray."*

*The officers helped me up, and the weight of what happened was heavy on my shoulders. As I fumbled with the lock, I saw Kar's muddy boots, standing like sentinels by the door, a small bouquet of flowers from the garden poking out from the top of one of them. That's when the tears began.*

---

WHEN THE POLICE FINALLY LEFT, I had called Val, and she came over immediately, being a rock for me when I needed her most. I convinced her to leave a few hours later, when I told her I'd be fine but really wanted to be alone for a while. I slept fitfully that night, thoughts of Kar invading my mind. We'd had had a good life together, and I was angry that he was taken from me.

I'd met Kar twenty years earlier at a gallery opening in Boston. I'd gone with Val, and while she was roaming, I found myself staring at a photograph by the featured artist, next to a handsome, white-haired gentleman.

"Intriguing, isn't it? See how the shadows play against each other, especially in that corner?" He pointed. That's how it began.

Later on, Val whispered to me, "You better get his name and number or better yet, go out to coffee or something. I'll be fine by myself on the T." At the time, we both lived in Brighton, and had taken the subway or T—local shorthand for the MBTA—to Newbury Street for the opening.

As it turned out, Karson Raycroft also lived in Brighton—he was a professor at Boston College—and after coffee, the three of us rode the T home together.

Kar and I dated for a couple of years before moving in together. Kar was only five years older than me but had gone gray in his early thirties. I was convinced we looked more like father and son than boyfriends and thought folks stared at us as a result, but Kar would say, "Fuck 'em, they're just jealous that the hot young guy snagged the hot grandpa!" He never failed to make me laugh.

By the time we decided to move in together, Kar had grown tired of teaching and secured a job as an academic editor for a book company he'd already done some work for. I was looking for a change of scenery, both at work and home, so I transferred to another pharmacy in the suburbs where we found our dream home—out of the city, with plenty of space for Kar to indulge his love of gardening.

We spent most of our time together. Sure, we had some friends—Val especially—but we truly enjoyed each other's company. We began a tradition of ending most nights with a drink together. Kar taught me to enjoy bourbon, and we'd usually have some to end our day. One fall, Kar discovered how delicious it was when you mixed bourbon with apple cider. This led to an experiment once winter began.

"What if," Kar asked, "we combined some hot apple cider with the bourbon for a hot toddy?"

Upon further tasting, we both agreed that a splash of Fireball added just the right amount of cinnamon to the mix, and our new winter drink was born.

"You know," he told me one day, mug raised up in a toast, "you're just like this drink—hot and sweet. I love you, Toddy." And I found myself with a new nickname.

*I love you too, Kar. I've never stopped.*

I missed my time with Kar so much! We loved each other fiercely. That's partly why I still feel angry after all these years. He shouldn't have been taken from me so soon.

## seven

KAR

"HELLO, MY NAME IS KARSON," I said, addressing the semitransparent gentleman staring at me from across the street. That was one of the first things I learned when I realized I was deceased. I could see through other souls roaming around, and their overall coloring was muted. Almost grayed out. What I thought of as the 'real' world looked like it had when I was alive, except plants— trees, grass, flowers, and such seemed even more vibrant to me.

"Hi, Karson," he replied. "I'm Joseph. Have you been wandering long?"

"No, only for a few weeks." Wandering seemed like as good a term as any to describe what we were doing.

"Ah, a newcomer. Welcome." He smiled. "I've been here for over seven years if I remember correctly."

"Wow, that's quite a long time. May I ask how you keep

track of your time here? I met someone when I first arrived, and she said it was difficult for her to remember."

"Frankly, I find it rather easy if you don't focus on individual days or weeks," he told me. "I estimate the time by the seasons. Thankfully, we're in New England instead of someplace like Florida, where every day is more or less the same. Plus, on the anniversary of your passing, you'll feel something pulling you, usually toward the east. That's what I call the universe reminding you that you should be moving on," he explained. "I focus on both the seasons and that pulling feeling to keep tabs on things."

"That's quite interesting," I remarked. "May I ask why you're still, um, wandering after all these years? Why haven't you moved on yet?"

"I just don't feel ready yet. It's hard to explain." He sighed. "I've met others who say that the pulling feeling is overwhelming, and they just have to go, but it's not been that strong for me. Maybe I'm supposed to do something first." He shook his head. "I don't really know, but I figure when it's my time, I'll head east."

"I understand," I said to him. "I feel the same way. I believe I'm here for a reason, and eventually I'll know what that is." We ambled along, no actual destination in mind, but he seemed content to just walk and chat.

"You seem quite comfortable here for someone who's only been wandering for a few weeks. Many newcomers tend to be rather frantic," he commented.

"Hmmm," I replied. "I don't know why that is, except that as I said, I get the feeling that I'm still here for a reason, so why not just go with it, right? Getting all anxious won't help, so why bother?"

"Makes sense, I suppose."

"Since you've been here for a while, do you mind if I ask you something?"

"Not at all," Joseph said.

"Do you have any advice for me? Something you think I should know?"

"Well," he began, "I'm sure you've already figured out that you don't need to sleep. I've found that libraries can be quite interesting places in the middle of the night. I've read so many books when no one else is there."

"But how can you do that? My hand passes right through whatever I've tried to touch." I was intrigued at this news.

"Ah, well, then," he said, eyes seeming to sparkle. "Come with me, my friend, and I'll teach you how you can manipulate things in the real world."

———

EVENTUALLY, we arrived at a deserted field on the edge of town, and Joseph sat me down in an area that was sparsely covered in grass and weeds. He pointed to a small pebble and said, "Watch closely." I stared in amazement as he pushed the pebble, and it rolled a few inches.

"How the hell did you do that?" I nearly shouted.

"It takes concentration and motivation." He smiled brightly. "Watch again."

It took me quite a while, but I slowly got the hang of it. When I finally succeeded, Joseph was gleeful.

"Well done, my friend!" he exclaimed. "But keep practicing whenever you have the chance, and it will become easier. You'll also be able to move larger items if you focus enough."

"This is amazing. I can't thank you enough for teaching me."

"But a word of warning," he cautioned. "If you interact with the physical world too much, you will feel something akin to fatigue. A little rest will remedy that, though."

"That's helpful to know," I said.

"When I first began my treks to the library, I'd take a book from a shelf and place it on a table. Then I'd need to rest a bit before actually opening it. But now I can do it with ease. And turning the pages takes almost no energy at all."

"This is all fascinating. I'm so grateful," I told him.

We parted ways shortly after that, but he informed me that he spent a lot of his time in a particular neighborhood not far from where we were. He didn't say more, but I suspected someone close to him in life was in the vicinity. No matter where I wandered, I tended to stay close to the house where I'd lived with Beck.

"You know where to find me if you have any more questions," he said, waving as he walked away.

———

Before meeting Joseph, I had to admit, my days had been rather monotonous. I'd wander around, observing people and the occasional spirit—most of them would look at me curiously, then hurry away—but frankly, there wasn't much to do. And nights were the worst. I no longer slept, so most of the time I'd just sit somewhere and wait until daylight. I was bored.

But the encounter with Joseph changed all of that. Once the sun set, I'd head to the closest library and wait for it to close. When everyone was gone, I'd pick a book and read until sunrise. I found that I didn't need much in the way of light in order to see the pages although sitting near a window where a streetlight or the moon shone through certainly helped. I read the occasional novel but found most of my solace in the gardening section. There I pored over every volume, relishing each word and picture.

A while after my initial meeting with Joseph, I was surprised to find him waving at me as I ambled down the street one day, intending to visit what was once my home. I liked to check in frequently, mostly just to look at Beck. *God, how I missed him.*

"Hello, Karson," Joseph called out to me.

We strolled together, catching up on what we'd been up to since our last encounter.

"Thank you again," I told him, "for showing me how to interact with things in the real world. I spend most of my evenings in a library now. I can't tell you how much I enjoy reading again."

"Glad I was able to help," he replied. "I haven't been around here for a while. I went to Dublin for a while. Needed a change of scenery."

"What do you mean, you went to Dublin?" I asked. I couldn't imagine how a spirit could travel to such a destination. "How it that possible?"

Jospeh looked at me askance. "Don't you know that you can transport yourself to anywhere you've been before?"

"No!" I practically shouted. "How would I know that? Did someone forget to give me the handbook explaining all of this?" I winked at him.

"I'm sorry, Karson," he said softly. "I thought you knew. Let me explain."

He proceeded to tell me how, by concentrating on a place that you knew well, you could will yourself to that place.

"Go on," he said once he'd finish with the explanation.

"Pick a place close by that we both know and try it. I'll meet you there."

"How about the corner of Spruce and Main?" I suggested. It was a few blocks away, and there was a park on one of the blocks there.

"Perfect," he said. "The corner where the bench and lamp-post are. Okay, you first."

I concentrated hard on the spot, picturing it in my mind and focusing on being there. Suddenly, I felt a stirring of air around me, and then I was standing right in front of the bench. A moment later, Joseph appeared a few feet away.

"That was amazing!" I exclaimed.

"But remember, it does take some personal energy to accomplish this. The farther you travel, the more energy it uses, so you may feel fatigued once you arrive. But some rest will take care of that."

"Thank you again, Joseph," I said sincerely. "Once again, you've improved my existence here."

# eight

BECK

ANOTHER UNEVENTFUL WEEK HAD PASSED, and once we were done with work on Friday, I met Val at Fiddler's for dinner and a drink or two.

"So, no more weird incidents at home?" Val asked. We were sitting at the far end of the bar, sipping our beverages.

"Nothing," I replied. "If not for the fact that I saved that bouquet of wildflowers, I would suspect I had imagined it all."

"Have you given any more thought to what we talked about after you read those articles?"

"Not really," I admitted. "Things have quieted down, so I'm not sure there's much more to say on the subject." Part of me hated to burst Val's bubble, but I was still having a hard time thinking about this paranormal stuff, especially when the anniversary of Kar's death was so close. "I'm sorry, Val, but I don't really want to talk about this right now. Can we change the subject, please?"

"Fine," she said softly. I think she understood that it was a difficult time for me, so she didn't press. "Let me tell you about this book I just finished. It's the first in a series, and I think you'd like it."

We began an in-depth discussion of the new book. It was the first in a cozy mystery series by author Gregory Ashe. By the time we'd finished our meal, I'd used my phone to buy the first book in the series for my Kindle.

———

IT WAS STILL FAIRLY EARLY when I got home. Val and I no longer stayed out until all hours like we had in college, but I wasn't all that tired, so I poured myself a nightcap and sat in my recliner. Opening my Kindle, I started reading the book I'd purchased earlier.

As much as I was enjoying this new story, after a few chapters, my eyelids began to droop. I padded up to my bedroom where I undressed, took care of business in the en suite bathroom, then shuffled to the king-sized bed.

I paused, noticing something on my pillow. Moving closer, I realized it was a small bundle of flowers—I knew they were blooms that grew in the side garden, but except for the black-eyed Susans and a couple of daisies, I couldn't identify the specific kinds.

I began to tremble, my heart pounding, and a shriek built in my throat until it burst forth. *What the fuck was happening?*

I sat in the upholstered chair in the corner of the room, trying desperately to slow my heart and relax. After several minutes, I felt more in control and grabbed my phone from the dresser where I'd left it earlier.

"Oh God, it happened again!" I shouted when Val picked up.

"Tell me what happened." She was a calm port for the storm that was still raging in my mind.

I explained everything, desperately trying to keep the fear out of my voice. I failed miserably at the end, breaking down into sobs. "Why is this happening? Is it really Kar, or am I losing my mind? Why now? Did I do something to cause this?" I was babbling but couldn't stop myself.

"Easy, Beck," Val said gently. "It's gonna be okay. We'll figure out what's going on."

"But how can ... um, I mean, are you sure?" I stammered.

"Do you trust me?"

"Of course," I answered honestly.

"I might know someone who can help. Let me talk to them, and I'll let you know."

"Okay. Thanks, Val." I ended the call and retreated to the guest bedroom. There was no way I could sleep in my bed tonight. Once again, it was a long time before I fell asleep.

———

I woke cranky, having tossed and turned more than actually slept the night before. But I had things to do, so after a quick breakfast, including lots of caffeine, I made a list—groceries, pick up dry cleaning, get a few things at the liquor store—then I set off, mentally determining the best route to take to get everything done in record time. I knew I'd need a nap that afternoon.

I was carrying the last of the bags in from my car when my cell rang.

"Hey, Val. What's up?"

"I wanted to see how you were doing today."

"If you must know, shitty, but it is what it is."

"I'm sorry. I know this is difficult for you." Her tone was sincere.

"But I ran some errands this morning, and I think it helped clear some of the cobwebs from my brain."

"I wanted to let you know that I called my friend Tony. He owns the Raven's Claw. I think he might know someone who can help you."

"That's the new-age shop, right?" I asked. "Books, candles, tarot cards, and things."

"Yeah," Val replied. "Tony's a good guy, and like I said, he might know someone. Anyway, I left a message. I'll explain the situation once I hear back from him. I'll call you when I know more."

"Thanks, Val. I appreciate it."

I put the groceries away and reheated some leftover soup for lunch. I retired to the guest room once again for a nap. While I'd gone into my bedroom that morning to grab some clothes, I avoided the bed although I could still see the flowers on my pillow.

I woke to the sound of my phone ringing again.

"Val," I answered groggily. "What's up?"

"Shit, I woke you, didn't I?"

"It's fine. I've been sleeping for a couple of hours, so I'm glad you called. If I slept any longer, I'd be awake all night." I stood and shuffled down the stairs to my den.

"Tony called me back," Val said. "I told him what's been going on."

"And? Can he help?" I still wasn't sure I actually believed in any of this, but I needed answers.

"He knows someone who deals with things like this. His

name is Travis Watson, and he's got a talent for speaking with the dead. I guess you'd call him a medium."

"You mean like that woman on the old TV show?" I tried very hard to keep the skepticism out of my voice.

"Something like that," Val admitted. "Tony gave me his number. He says he thinks Travis can help you. What do you want to do?"

"I guess it wouldn't hurt to talk to him. Can you please call him, explain a little of what's going on, and ask him to come out to the house? Oh, and Val, I really want you to be here too. Is that okay?"

"Of course, Beck. I'll call him now and make the arrangements."

I was partly relieved, partly apprehensive about what would happen. Would I get the answers I so desperately needed—and was somewhat afraid to hear—or was this a huge waste of time?

# nine

I MANEUVERED my old Honda Accord up the long driveway and parked behind an SUV. I figured that was Valerie's vehicle since she had made it clear she'd be at this meeting too. As I walked to the porch, I glanced around, trying to get a sense of the place. It was a well-maintained and landscaped lot surrounding a beautiful Craftsman-style home. Flowers and shrubs surrounded the home in a pleasing display, and I noticed a large wildflower garden on one side.

I attempted to open my senses to the area. Could I sense a spirit lingering there? There was *something*. As if someone *had* been here but wasn't now.

Shortly after I rang the doorbell, an extremely handsome man—I judged him to be a couple of years older than my forty-five years—opened the door.

"Mr. Watson?" he asked. When I nodded, he gestured for me to enter. "I'm Beckett Gray. Please come in."

"Nice to meet you, Mr. Gray. Please, call me Travis." Beckett was about my height, perhaps an inch or so taller, so I'd put him at six-one. I was immediately drawn to his piercing blue eyes.

"Beck," he said kindly, offering his hand. We shook. I felt a tingle when our hands met. *Hmmm, that's interesting.* "And you know Val." A woman stood in the foyer.

"Ah, we've never formally met in person, but I do remember seeing you at Tony's shop a couple of times."

"Nice to finally meet you, Travis," she said. "Tony speaks well of you."

I followed them down the hall into a room that I guessed was a den or study. In addition to a desk and some bookcases, there was a recliner in front of the rear window and a sofa with two plush chairs that formed a sitting area around a low table.

"I believe Val has explained what's been going on," Beck began. "Do you have any questions?"

"I'd like a little background if you don't mind," I said. I pulled a small brown leather notebook from my jacket pocket. The cover was worn from many years of use. "Is it all right if I take a few notes?"

"Sure," Beck replied. "What is it you want to know?"

"I understand that your husband died, and you think this may be somehow related. Exactly how long ago did he die?"

"Almost five years ago. The anniversary of his death is coming up soon." I detected strong emotion in Beck's voice. He clearly cared a lot for his deceased spouse.

"Was there anything unusual about his death? Any strange occurrences when he passed?"

"He was struck ..." Beck trailed off, seemingly overcome with grief.

He nodded at Val, and she continued. "Beck's husband,

Karson, was struck and killed by a hit-and-run driver one afternoon while he was jogging. It happened just down the road from here," she said quietly.

"Oh!" This revelation surprised me. "I'm so very sorry. I had no idea." Beck's reaction to his husband's death touched my soul, and I felt an enormous amount of compassion for this man.

Val looked at Beck. "Do you need some water, hun?" she asked him. He shook his head.

"Am I correct that there hasn't been any type of paranormal activity until now?" I asked.

"That's correct," Beck answered. "And I must be honest with you up front. I'm not entirely sure I believe in all this paranormal activity as you call it." His voice wasn't bitter, but there was certainly an edge to it. "Although thanks to Val, I will admit I'm beginning to come around."

"I understand, Beck." I told him. "Many people have trouble believing, but I can tell you, I've seen and heard many things that defy explanation. I promise to do my best to help you come to terms with whatever is going on."

"Thank you. I guess that's all I can ask."

"From what Val told me on the phone, there have been a few different manifestations, correct?" Beck nodded, and I continued. "Can you show me where? And tell me exactly what you saw?"

Beck and Val took me to the front porch and foyer, then to the kitchen, and finally to Beck's bedroom on the second floor. He explained what he had seen in each case, even telling me that he'd kept the flowers from the front porch, placing them in a vase on the kitchen island. The more I watched and listened to him, the stronger my attraction became. I wasn't used to feeling this way about someone so quickly, but there was something very special about Beckett Gray.

When we returned to the den, I said, "We have instances of physical manifestations—like the flowers from the front porch and the ones on your pillow, as well as what I call metaphysical or mystical manifestations. That would be the muddy footprints that you saw, but later when you went back to them, they were gone," I explained. "They were never physically there, but you were meant to see them and believed them to be real."

"So these things really happened?" Beck asked. "I'm not going crazy?"

"I believe they actually happened. And no, I don't think you're going crazy," I told him. "Everything you described are things that I've seen and heard about before. Spirits with enough determination can certainly cause those things to happen."

"So what happens next?" Val asked. "Can you contact this spirit? Find out if it's really Kar and ask him why these things are happening now?"

"I can most likely contact the spirit, but it's not something I can do now. I've been keeping a psychic eye, if you will, on the surroundings, and while I know that a spirit has been here recently, I don't sense them here now," I told them. "Here's what I'd like to suggest. Beck, put my contact number in your phone. The next time something happens, call me—any time of the day or night—and I'll come over. I need to be able to feel this spirit's presence more strongly so that I can try to reach out to them. How does that sound?"

"Sure, I can do that," Beck said. "I do have one more question."

"Of course."

"Not to be crass, but how much is this gonna cost?"

I named an amount and explained it included the initial consult plus doing what I could to rid the house of the spirit if that's ultimately what he wanted.

"What do you mean, if that's what I want? I thought that was the point of all this?" He sounded a little confused. *Jeez, he's adorable when his face scrunches up like that!*

"In my experience, when some folks learn that it is indeed a loved one who is hanging around, they actually decide to let them stay," I explained. "It's the unknown aspect that was bothering them, but they're happy to let the spirit linger once they know for sure who they are."

"Oh, I um, well, I don't expect that to be the case here," Beck said softly.

———

I THOUGHT about our meeting on my drive home.

Beckett Gray was a most interesting man. Quite handsome with that dark hair and those deep, almost brooding eyes. He didn't smile often in our meeting, but when he did, his entire face lit up, and I saw something in his visage. Hope, perhaps? He said he wasn't sure he believed, but yet he thought I could help. So yes, there had definitely been hope there.

Was the spirit of his dead husband trying to reach out for some reason? I believed it was likely although why it had taken almost five years for Karson to attempt this contact was somewhat confusing to me. But for the moment, that didn't matter. If I could communicate with Karson, I could probably find out and relay that info to Beck.

Yes, I would certainly do everything I could to help Beck with this situation. Plus, I'd love another excuse to see the man.

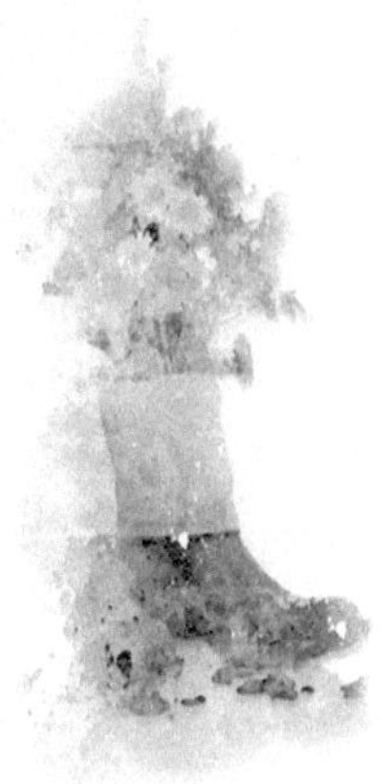

# ten

BECK

"So what do you think?" Val asked me after Travis had left.

"He's not exactly what I expected," I answered honestly.

"I don't know what that means."

"Well, it's just that he looked rather ordinary. Not as, um, well, 'mystical' as I expected." I air quoted.

"What, you expected him to wear a black cape and be sporting a sinister mustache he could twirl at the ends?" Val's voice raised in pitch.

"No, don't be ridiculous. It's just, I dunno, he was wearing jeans and a leather jacket. Although he *was* also wearing those small stones around his neck. Plus, he was younger than I expected. I pictured someone older and less handsome." *I* felt like the ridiculous one as I spoke those words.

"You thought he was handsome?" Val stared. "Since when

do you notice something like that? What's going on in that brain of yours?"

"C'mon," I scoffed, "didn't you find that dark hair and beard with those chocolate-brown eyes the least bit attractive?" *Wait. Why was I suddenly thinking about how attractive Travis was? Val was right, I didn't normally notice those things.*

"Well ..." Val started.

"I don't like where this conversation is going," I admitted. "Do you think he'll be able to do anything for me?"

"As I told Travis, Tony says good things about him," Val replied. I was grateful that she didn't press me on my previous comments. "I think it's certainly worth trying. You need answers, and he believes he can provide them. And for your information, those stones, as you call them, are crystals. I recognized a couple of them. They offer protection and can enhance one's psychic abilities."

"Okay, good to know. I just hope I don't have to wait too long before something else happens." My stomach knotted. *Was I really hoping for more mysterious happenings? Well, if it meant getting answers, I guess I was.*

"I'm sure it will all work out. I'm gonna head home, but I'll see you at work in the morning."

"Night, Val." We hugged, and I kissed her temple. I waited at the door until I saw her drive away.

I hadn't wanted to admit it to Val, but yes, I had found Travis Watson a very attractive man. And Val was right, I didn't normally take note of something like that. So what changed this time?

———

IT WAS ALMOST a week later when the next physical manifestation, as Travis had called it, occurred.

After spending a quiet evening at home, I retired to my bedroom—yes, I had cleared away the flowers, changed the linens, and was sleeping in my own bed again—and changed into sleep pants and an old T-shirt. Before I slipped under the covers, something shiny caught my eye on the dresser to my right. I moved toward it, curious but also afraid of what it might be. It was Kar's wedding ring.

I quickly backed away. *How on earth did it get there?* I kept it in a small jewelry case in the top drawer along with several other pieces that Kar had worn. I *knew* I hadn't looked in that case for months.

Grabbing my phone from the nightstand, I called Travis.

"Hello?" he said sleepily.

"Travis? It's Beckett Gray. I'm sorry, did I wake you?"

"No, it's fine. I dozed off in front of the TV. What's wrong?"

"Something happened. A physical manifestation is what you called it," I told him. "I was getting ready for bed when I noticed Kar's wedding ring on the dresser, but I didn't put it there. I keep it in a case in a drawer."

"Okay. Have you moved it?" he asked.

"No. I backed away and called you."

"Good. Don't touch it. I'll be there in about twenty minutes." He ended the call.

———

I WAITED FOR TRAVIS DOWNSTAIRS, sitting on the stairs in the foyer until I heard his car pull into the driveway.

"Thanks for coming," I said, letting him in. He followed

me upstairs and into the bedroom. From the doorway, I pointed to the ring, still sitting on the dresser, and he nodded.

He stood near the dresser, closed his eyes, and held his hand out, palm facing the ring as if trying to feel something from it. "Yes," he whispered. "There's definitely someone here."

"Is it—"

"Shhh. Don't say anything, please," he said quietly. "Karson Raycroft, are you here?" he called in a strong voice. Travis looked around the room as if searching for someone. At one point, he stopped and stared, then continued to take in the entire space.

At first nothing happened. Then after a minute or two, the ring moved about two inches to the left.

"How ..." I started, my mouth agape.

"Karson," Travis said again. "Is that you?"

I felt a breeze move past me as if someone had walked by quickly.

Travis turned to me. "He's gone. But before he left, I heard something in my head. A faint voice said, 'Yes.' I believe it was Karson, but he sounded very tired."

I put my hand out to steady myself against the doorframe but missed. I tumbled to the floor.

———

I WOKE, staring into warm brown eyes. Travis's face slowly came into focus. "What happened?"

"You fainted," he replied seriously. "Here, let me help you up."

I stood on shaky legs, but Travis held my arm firmly and supported my back. Despite my unease at what had just happened, I had to admit it felt good to be held by someone again.

"Do you want to sit?" Travis asked me, nodding to the overstuffed chair in the corner.

"Can we go downstairs, please?"

"Do you want a glass of water?" Concern colored his words. He hovered over me as I sat on the sofa in the den.

"I think I'd like something stronger," I told him. "You'll find some bourbon in the farthest cabinet to the right. Glasses are there too." I pointed toward the kitchen. After a few moments, I heard the ice dispenser, and he soon returned with a short tumbler filled with ice and a bottle of Woodford Reserve.

"Here ya go." He placed the items on the coffee table.

"You can join me if you'd like." I poured a generous amount into my glass.

"Thanks, but I'll pass." He had an odd look on his face, so I didn't press.

"How do you do this and not go crazy?"

He smiled and said, "Who says I'm not?"

I barked out a laugh. "Touché."

"Seriously, though, I guess I'm just used to it now. I can't remember a time when I didn't hear the voices of spirits or sense something about a person."

"So that really was Karson upstairs just now?" My breath quickened. Did I really want to know?

"If the voice I heard is to be believed, then yes, it was," he said honestly. "And I have no reason to doubt it. Although it was faint, it was clearly a mature male voice."

"What happens now?" I sipped at my bourbon.

"I'd hoped to be able to talk to him more, but I felt him

leave," he told me. "Actually, he sounded tired, which is understandable."

I was confused. "How can a ghost be tired?"

"When spirits interact with the physical world, like Karson did by getting the ring out of its case and putting it on the dresser, it takes energy. And he used more energy when we saw the ring move. Depending on what else he may have done today, energy use will tire him out. But don't worry, he'll get stronger once he rests for a while."

"I don't mean to sound skeptical, but how do you know all of this?"

"Well, I've spoken to many spirits over the years, and a few of them have been forthcoming with information," he replied.

"You said you had hoped to talk to him. Were you gonna ask him to leave?"

"First I wanted to find out why he was doing all of this now," Travis said. "You told me that you hadn't seen any manifestations in the past, so I'm curious why it's all starting now. It seems clear that Karson has been roaming around for almost five years but hasn't tried to make contact before."

"Are you still gonna be able to do that?"

"Yes, but not tonight. I no longer sense him in the house, so I'll need to come back and try again."

"Okay." I kept my voice neutral. I'd hoped to know more tonight, but I resigned myself to the fact that this would take more time. "It's late, and I don't want to keep you. Thank you again for coming. I'll let you know if or when anything else happens."

# eleven

"So tell me again about Auntie Mae," I said to Tony. We were sitting in my living room. "She's not really your aunt, right?"

"No, she isn't," he answered. "Remember how I told you that I came to live with my nan after my folks died?" Tony had been born to a British dad and an American mom just outside of London and moved to the US when he was just seven after his parents had been killed in a bizarre skiing accident.

"Sure. Your grandmother raised you and left you the Raven's Claw."

"Right. Well, Nan introduced me to Auntie Mae when I was about ten years old. Nan called her Auntie Mae, and so that's how I've always addressed her. I have no idea whose aunt she is, she's just Auntie Mae. Why, may I ask, this sudden interest?"

"I may actually be ready to meet her," I admitted.

"Really? I'm happy since I think she might be able to help you, but why now?"

"It's that job you told me about. Remember, you asked me to call Valerie Grimes? It seems it's her friend that's experiencing the spirit activity."

"Did she tell you what kind of activity?" Tony sounded concerned. "She spoke in rather broad terms when I talked to her."

"Yeah. Some physical manifestations like muddy footprints and flowers mysteriously appearing. Apparently, this guy's husband passed away almost five years ago, and this activity just started recently. I've been to the house twice now. The first time, the entity wasn't there, but I definitely felt something. The second time, I made brief contact, but the spirit left pretty quickly."

"And you think Auntie Mae can help? She really doesn't deal with helping spirits move along anymore," Tony said.

"Actually, I'm hoping she can help *me*. I feel a bit out of my league with this one. I'm not sure I can explain it. Just something feels 'off,' but yet I want to help. I think if Auntie Mae can help me better understand this gift I have, I'll be more effective overall."

"Okay, I'll talk to Auntie Mae and see if I can set up a time for the two of you to meet."

"Thanks, Tone."

"Hey, what are friends for?"

———

AUNTIE MAE WASN'T MERELY old, she was ancient. If I had to guess, I'd say she was in her late nineties. Maybe even older. Her mahogany skin was wrinkled beyond anything I'd seen.

Her long, snow-white hair was plaited into a single braid that trailed halfway down her back.

Despite her frail appearance, her topaz eyes were bright, and I immediately saw wisdom there. Her slight frame was clad in a patchwork of blue—more shades of the color than I could imagine.

She took my hand in a firm grasp—the strength behind it surprised me. I was unable to pull away. "You have a strong gift, Travis," she told me, staring into my eyes. "But much of it is wild, untrained. I can help you. But you must want it."

"I do, ma'am," I answered.

"Call me Auntie Mae, child," she replied. Turning to Tony, she said, "Leave us, son. What I have to say is not for your ears. Wait in the kitchen; there's tea and cookies there. When I call you, bring some in for Travis and me. But know that this may take a while."

After he left, she told me to sit across from her. "Now, child," she began. "Tony has told me what you do to help folks, and I can see with my inner eye what you're capable of. Frankly, I'm surprised you've survived this long without the training you need. Why were you not trained, dear boy?"

I explained to her how I had grown up, not wanting this gift and balking at much of what my gran had tried to teach me.

"Pfft," she scolded. "The young have no patience. Your gran was only trying to prepare you for what was to come. I can help some, but it won't be easy now that you're older. Tell me what you do to prepare before you try to speak to a spirit or discern what is happening when you are called upon."

"Um, I'm not sure what you mean by prepare. I just try to concentrate on the presence that's there and ask them why they're there."

"But what about grounding yourself? Centering to protect yourself and the power you hold?" She sounded shocked.

"Grounding? Centering? Sorry, I don't know what that is," I confessed.

"But these are the fundamentals!" Auntie Mae practically shouted. "No wonder you're leaking power and always exhausted when you try to help. Well, no matter, what's done is done." Shaking her head, she continued, "We'll need to start at the beginning."

"Okay," I said tentatively, not exactly sure what she meant.

"Tell me, son, how difficult is it for you to make contact with the spirits?"

"Not difficult at all. I pretty much hear them all the time."

"How do you stop the chatter?" she asked.

"When it gets to be too much, I drink to try and mute them." I blushed. "It helps a little."

"Ah, child." Sadness tinged her words. "That's never a good thing." She shook her head, and for the first time in a long time, I was ashamed of what I had been doing. "But it's water under the bridge. No changing the past. I'll help you, Travis."

She told me to stand and relax, then imagine myself anchoring to the ground below me. I tried to do what she asked, but in a moment, I was knocked on my ass.

"What happened?" I was flabbergasted.

"I pushed you with my mind, child. And since you weren't properly grounded, you fell over," she explained. "Let's try again."

What seemed like hours passed. I was proving to be an awful, unteachable student. When I felt like giving up completely, she said, "I have another idea. Sit. Close your eyes and open your mind to me."

"I don't know how to—" I started.

"Ah, forget I said that. Just relax and try to listen inside your head."

After a moment, I heard something, but it was different. The sound felt like it was in my brain.

*It's me, Travis. It's Auntie Mae.*

"But how ..."

*NO. With your mind, not your mouth.*

*But how is this possible?* I asked in my head. *I've heard the voices of spirits in my head before, but I've never spoken in my head. And never to someone that's still alive.*

*It's the gift, child. It works both ways. Now imagine you can see me there. Picture me in your mind and watch what I do.*

I was fascinated by her actions in my head. I saw her take a deep breath, then what looked like roots began to flow from her head, surrounding her and anchoring themselves to the ground beneath her feet. I suddenly understood what she meant by grounding myself.

*Now you try it,* I heard her say.

I practiced until she was satisfied that I understood the lesson.

*Good, Travis. Remember, grounding can help you quiet the voices you hear. Now that you know how to ground, this is how you center yourself.* Once again, she showed me in my head what I needed to do. As I looked closely, I saw tendrils that seemed to ebb and flow from around her. I somehow knew that this was energy coming from her very being. Another deep breath, and what seemed to be invisible hands began to pull the energy back into herself so that nothing escaped. It was all so clear now, I didn't know how I had never figured that out before. I was quickly able to mimic her actions.

When she was again satisfied with what I had learned, she spoke aloud. "That's enough for today. You've done well." I beamed at her compliment, finally beginning to understand some of the things that my gran had tried to teach me so long ago. "Tony," she called out. "Please bring the tea and cookies."

A few minutes later, Tony came in carrying a tray with a teapot, cups, and a plate of cookies. "I brewed a new pot, Auntie Mae," he said. "It's been almost two hours, and the tea had gone cold."

I was exhausted, feeling like I'd run a marathon, but the tea and cookies, both laced with sugar, helped.

———

As I LAID in bed that evening, I thought about everything I'd learned from Auntie Mae that day. She'd explained that without grounding and centering myself, extra power would leak out as I used it, and some spirits could actually grab that power to strengthen themselves. The power leak was why I got tired as easily as I did, but grounding and centering would stop most of that from happening now.

She went on to explain that this was just the beginning. I still had lots to learn, and after seeing how I did with my first lesson, she was willing to continue to help me. I breathed a sigh of relief. If it meant that I could do my job and help people without hearing voices all the time, I was more than willing to try.

# twelve

KARSON

I stood at the spot where I had died. I couldn't believe that almost five years had passed since that fateful day. The sadness I originally felt had been replaced by a longing for closure. When it first happened, I couldn't understand why my spirit lingered here, but I never felt that overwhelming need to move on. In the beginning, I thought perhaps I was mourning the end of my life and the fact that there were still things I'd never get to do.

Oh, how I wished Beck and I had traveled more! We talked about going to France and England, Greece and Italy. But we always put things off, thinking we'd do those things once we were retired. Fate had different plans for us.

The more time I spent in this interim plane, the more I realized that I was hanging around to make sure that Beck was okay. My death hit him hard, and he mourned my passing for a long time. Thank God Val was around to help him keep going.

I don't know what would have happened to him if she hadn't been there to hold him together.

But as time moved forward, I began to realize that Beck wasn't really living, he was just existing—going through the motions if you will. All he did was work and occasionally go out with Val. In the first year or so after I died, he would speak to some of our friends on the phone but never accepted any of their invitations, and those calls soon stopped. He never showed an interest in anyone else, never dated, never really moved on.

The Beck I knew, the man I fell in love with, was a vibrant soul who loved life and enjoyed doing things. Even though we never traveled outside of the country, we spent many weekends in nearby Boston or on Cape Cod, even heading to New York on a few occasions. We went to the theater, dined at various restaurants, went to clubs and concerts. Sometimes alone but often with friends. We had lived a full life together. And that all changed when I died. It pained me to see him like this.

Recently, it dawned on me that I was still here because I needed to help Beck find a way to move on with his life. Once I did that, I'd be able to move on with my, well, with my death, I guess.

———

I WAS STROLLING through a nearby park one day, thinking about what I could do to help my still-living husband find another person to love. He wasn't even fifty yet, and there was no reason he couldn't enjoy the rest of his life with another person.

"Hello, Karson," I heard a voice call out, startling me out of my musings. I turned to see Joseph heading my way.

"Hi, Joseph," I replied. We'd not seen each other for quite some time. "It's been a while. I started to wonder if maybe you'd moved on."

"I've thought about it," he said honestly. "But I just have a feeling that there's still something I must do before I go. And what about you? You've been here a while now. No desire to move on?"

"It's been nearly five years," I admitted. "But the realization of what I need to do before I move on just came to me the other day. Now it's a matter of figuring out how to do it."

"Why don't you tell me about it?" Joseph said. "Perhaps I can help."

We sat by some trees near the small pond in the center of the park, and I explained to him what I thought I needed to do.

"So you want to help your husband find love again," he recapped. "I must say, that's a new one. Most spirits that I've met have a difficult time thinking of their spouses with someone else."

"I'd love to still be with him, but since that's not possible, I just want him to be happy again."

"I think that's admirable," Joseph said. "I have a couple of ideas that might help. But first I need to know something. Have you tried contacting Beck yet? Does he know you're here?"

"No," I admitted. "I've visited him many times. Just to keep an eye on him, you know? But he's never done anything that leads me to believe he knows I'm there."

"The fact is, most people can't see or hear us. There are some folks who are sensitive to our energy, but they are few and far between. It will take some type of manifestation to get Beck's attention."

"You mean like moving an item? I supposed I could do that."

"You could do something like that, but rather than a physical manifestation, you might want to consider something else."

"I'm not sure what you mean," I admitted.

"Working with the energy from this plane, it's possible to create an illusion of sorts. I've heard others describe it as a mystical manifestation."

"Please tell me more," I implored him.

"Is there something that would convince Beck that you were there for him?"

"Yeah." I chuckled. "Back when I was still alive, I'd spend a fair amount of time out in my garden. I'd wear these gardening boots that would always end up covered in mud. If Beck saw muddy boot prints on the porch or in the front hall, he'd know. He was always reminding me to take my boots off at the door when I finished gardening."

"Perfect," Joseph replied. "Now remember how I told you to concentrate on an object that you want to actually move?" I nodded, and he continued. "You need to concentrate in the same way, but while you're doing that, imagine those muddy prints on the porch. Or in the foyer. In fact, try it now."

We moved closer to the pond, where there was a small clearing on one side. I did as he asked, imagining the tread of my gardening boots and the pattern they formed when I walked. Before too long, I saw footprints before me.

"That's it!" Joseph exclaimed. "Just like that. And the bonus is that this doesn't take nearly as much energy as moving physical items does. Once you've created the illusion, it should last for a few hours before it vanishes."

And thus began my plan to let Beck know that I was there for him.

———

I'd been at it for a few weeks now, trying both mystical and physical manifestations to convince Beck I was there. But my husband proved himself to be more stubborn than I remembered. Sure, he saw the things I did, but the first few times, he refused to believe it was me. When he finally spoke to Val about it, I knew he was starting to take it all seriously.

Then he surprised me. One day while he was out, I took my wedding band from the case where he kept it and placed it on the dresser. It took a bit more energy than I expected, having to open the drawer, extract the ring, and then close the drawer, but I was convinced it would be worth it.

When he saw the ring, he did something unexpected—he called someone. At first I thought it was Val, but a man showed up shortly after he made the call. He was good-looking, and I estimated him to be around Beck's age, but there was something else about him. I couldn't put my finger on it at first, but I somehow knew he was different. We were all standing in Beck's bedroom. The bedroom I once shared with him, but, well ...

I felt a power building. I realized it was coming from this stranger. Beck had called him Travis. He called out my name and scanned the room. At one point he stopped, looking right at me, then he moved on. Ah. I realized this was one of those special people that could make contact with spirits like me. *This is quite interesting.* To prove that I was indeed there, I moved the ring just an inch or two. I tried to answer Travis and managed to choke out a quiet "yes" when he asked if I was there, but I was suddenly overwhelmed with fatigue. Apparently, I'd overdone it, manipulating the ring as much as I had.

I was, however, excited that Beck had solicited the help of someone more capable. It was at that point that I left them, vowing to return another day and make better contact with Beck and Travis. Besides, there was something very special about this man, Travis. I could feel it in my very core. Perhaps he would turn out to be the person that Beck needed in his life.

# thirteen

BECK

I DRAGGED myself into work the next morning, feeling cranky and out of sorts.

Val took one look at me and said, "You look like shit! What's wrong? Did something happen last night?"

"Good morning to you." I chuckled, not feeling it at all. "And to answer your question, yes, something happened last night. I found Kar's wedding ring on my dresser. I have no idea how it got there. Well, that's not exactly true. I guess Kar put it there for me to find. At least that's what Travis thinks."

"Travis? You actually called him?" Val sounded incredulous. "I'm happy but surprised. I kind of thought you agreed to call him just to appease me."

"Yes, I called him. And he said Kar was there. Heard him say 'yes' when Travis asked if it was him," I said quietly. "But then, just like that—I snapped my fingers—"he was gone. Travis suspected that moving the ring took a lot of Kar's energy, and he was probably quite tired. He's hoping that something else happens, and he can make better contact with Kar to learn more about why he's doing all of this."

"Well," Val said, "at least it's a start. You'll call him the next time something happens, right?"

"Yes," I told her. Not only would I have another chance to contact Kar, but I'd get a chance to see Travis again. *What is it that I find so fascinating about him?*

———

THE REST of the week passed quickly, and before I knew it, I was waking up on Saturday morning with no further signs of Kar's presence. If I was being honest, I was disappointed. Part of me wanted—no, *needed*—to know why Kar was here. And the other part of me? For some reason, I found myself wanting to spend time with Travis. There was a calmness that surrounded him, and I wanted to be a part of that. I wanted to see the corners of his eyes crinkle when he smiled. *What is wrong with me? I've never thought about someone else like this. I still love Kar, don't I?*

I shook myself out of those thoughts and got ready for the day. After breakfast, I quickly finalized my shopping list and headed out. Somehow my regular Saturday routine—running errands, shopping for groceries—helped settle me. That was important, especially this weekend. Val had taken Friday and Monday off to have a sisters' weekend in New York, so that had meant no Fiddler's the night before for dinner and drinks. Sure, I could have gone alone, but it just wasn't the same.

Upon my return home from running errands, I changed into sweats and sat at my desk to do some writing. Or at least some planning. After Kar died, I saw a therapist for a while. I needed help to work through what was going on in my head as I mourned. When I told him I'd done some writing in the past, he recommended I try again, as it often proved to be an effective way to work through the grieving process.

I now had countless notebooks and computer files filled with unfinished stories. It seemed that no matter how I began a new story, it always ended up a tale of grief or death. Recently, though, I began toying with the idea of writing other things again. I took a couple of online classes, read a book or two, and started a list of story ideas that didn't involve anyone dying.

I opened a new file on my laptop and began typing. Surprisingly, the words flowed. Before I knew it, a couple of hours had passed, and I was well into the second chapter of what I envisioned to be a romance. Specifically, a gay romance. I kept a stack of small notebooks in the bottom drawer of the desk, and I pulled one out, making notes about characters and places as I reread what I'd written. Feeling satisfied with my accomplishments, I saved the file and went off in search of something for dinner. I settled on a grilled cheese sandwich and some tomato soup—perfect comfort food for a cool autumn night.

I'd just sat in my recliner, anxious to get back into the mystery I was reading, when my phone rang.

"Hey, Val," I said. "Shouldn't you be out clubbing with the girls?"

"Hi, Beck. It's too early for that," she admonished. "We're actually just getting ready to go to dinner, and I thought I'd check in while I wait for Deb to finish putting on her makeup. Normally, I'd be beating you at cribbage or something, so I wanted to see how you were doing."

"In your dreams, Val." I chuckled. The reality was, she probably *would* be winning, but I'd never admit to that. "I'm doing well. Inspiration struck, and I actually started writing a new story today."

"Really? That's great!" I could hear the sincerity in her voice. No doubt about it, Val was my rock. "What's this one about?"

"It's a gay romance about an airline pilot and a guy he meets during a layover."

"Just make sure no one dies," she said softly. "Okay. Deb and Joyce are ready and giving me the stink eye, so I've gotta run. I'll tell you all about the trip on Tuesday. Love you!"

"Love you too. Tell them I said hi. Now go and enjoy yourselves."

I had no sooner ended the call with Val and picked up my Kindle when my phone rang again. *Hmmm, who else would be calling me on a Saturday night?*

# fourteen

TRAVIS

I WOKE QUITE EARLY for me, feeling out of sorts. It was barely six o'clock. Since meeting with Auntie Mae, I'd cut back on my drinking. And while I felt better about myself, I wasn't sleeping as much as I used to.

Plus, I hadn't heard from Beck in over a week. While I found it odd that the spirit of his husband hadn't done anything to garner Beck's attention, I was more disturbed by the fact that I longed to see Beck again. It was a different experience for me, this desire to spend time with someone.

I shook off the cobwebs and, over breakfast, decided to visit Tony at the Raven's Claw. Until I heard from Beck again, I had no pressing business, but perhaps Tony could help me get out of my funk.

As I drove to the shop, I thought about my life. For most of it, I'd been a loner. Not that I particularly liked being alone. But growing up, I was different, and as a result, I didn't have many friends. Or any, really, if I'm being honest. No one wanted to hang out with the weirdo who heard voices and saw things no one else could see. My abilities eventually led me to Tony and his shop—I'd learned that crystals could sometimes help me in my work—and he became the only real friend I had.

I stopped at the café two doors down from the Raven's Claw and picked up a coffee for me and tea for Tony.

"Good morning, Tone," I greeted him, walking through the front door. "I come bearing gifts."

"Thanks, mate," he replied, taking the proffered cup. "What brings you out so early on this fine Saturday morning?"

"No reason," I said softly. "Can't a guy just pop in and visit a friend?" I was still trying to decide if I wanted to tell Tony that I might be developing a real interest in Beck.

"I call bullshit," Tony countered. "You've got that look about you. Like you're hiding something." *Shit! I should know better than to try and keep something from him.*

"Well, it's about the guy with the dead husband who's come back."

"Oh yeah? What's going on? The dead guy hasn't gotten violent or anything, has he?"

"No, nothing like that," I told him. "It's just that, well, I find myself thinking a lot about Beckett. Um, that's the spouse that's still alive."

"Really? That's not like you, Travis. You *never* get close to people, especially a client."

"Tell me about it. But I dunno, something's different about this guy. Client or not, I can't stop thinking about him. And to make matters worse, I haven't heard from him in over a week."

"Hmmm, that's odd. I mean, that the spirit hasn't done

anything that would make him call you. You don't think the entity has decided to move on, do you?"

"I dunno. You know how difficult it is to try and predict what a spirit will do, but I didn't get that feeling from Karson —that's the dead husband—when I had the brief encounter with him last time. There was something, I can't really explain it, but it felt like he still needed to do something."

"Huh. I've got an idea." Tony's eyes lit up. "Why don't you call this Beckett guy? Just say you are checking in and hope to talk with him a bit more about Karson. Then invite him out for coffee or something. That way, you can learn a bit more about the dead guy and also see the guy you're apparently hung up on right now."

"That's actually a pretty great idea," I agreed.

———

*Should I call him now? I could wait a few days to see if I hear from him.*

I had been running this debate in my head for hours ever since I got home from Tony's shop just before lunch. It was now well past dinner time.

"Oh, to hell with it!" I exclaimed aloud to absolutely no one. Grabbing my phone off the kitchen island, I quickly dialed Beck's number.

"Hello, Beck. It's Travis," I said when he answered the call. "I hope I'm not catching you at a bad time."

"Not at all. Just sitting here reading."

"How are you?"

"Fine," Beck replied. "How are you doing?"

"I'm well, thanks. Listen, I hadn't heard anything from you

this past week, so I thought I'd check in." I hoped I didn't sound too lame.

"Well, nothing's happened that I'm aware of, so there was no reason to contact you."

"I was wondering if we might meet sometime soon?" I asked. *Might as well get this over with.* "I'd like to get a bit more background information about Karson."

"I suppose we could. I spent the day running some errands and doing a few things around the house, but I guess you could come by sometime tomorrow if that works for you."

"Actually, I was thinking more of meeting for coffee. Or perhaps lunch if you don't have plans."

"Well ..." Beck began.

"Please say yes. I could meet you anywhere that's convenient for you." I prayed I didn't sound too needy.

"Okay." Beck chuckled. "You've talked me into it. Lunch tomorrow. Do you know where Chadwick's is?"

"I do," I said, recognizing the name of a small restaurant on the outskirts of town. "I'll meet you there at twelve thirty." I ended the call, sighing in relief. *I can't believe I actually went through with it.*

---

I AM NOT A FANCY MAN. But still, I wanted to look presentable for my lunch date with Beck, so I took extra care with my appearance. After showering, I trimmed my short beard, which had gotten a bit unkempt over the past couple of weeks. And I actually used a bit of product in my hair. Now I stood, clad only in a towel, in front of my closet, trying to decide what to wear. I settled on black jeans with a cobalt-blue cotton sweater.

I arrived at the restaurant early. Part of me was anxious to see Beck again, but I also hated being late for anything. As a result, I sat in my car for about fifteen minutes and was still early when I walked into the place.

Beck arrived about ten minutes after I secured a table for us. He looked good. He was dressed casually in dark jeans and a gray pullover under a forest-green barn jacket with leather trim. We shook hands, and once again I felt a tingle when our hands touched. *Hmmm, there's that feeling again.*

"Thanks for agreeing to have lunch with me," I said in greeting.

"Not a problem. After all, we both have to eat, right?" Beck smiled.

We perused the menu for a few minutes, and after the server took our order, Beck turned to me. "On the phone yesterday, you told me you wanted some additional background on Kar. What is it exactly that you're looking for?"

"I'd just like to get a sense of who he was. Frankly, many spirits move on pretty quickly. It's rare for an entity to just hang around for years. I'm hoping if I know a bit more about him, I might be able to figure out why he's still roaming the temporary plane."

"So you're saying this isn't what usually happens?"

"When someone dies, their spirit exists on the temporary or interim plane," I explained. "They can still interact with this plane, the one where we live. But most entities don't remain there very long. They tend to move on to another plane of existence, where they no longer have any real contact with our world. At least, that's what I've been told."

"Okay. I can tell you about Kar, but first I have a question for you."

"Of course. What would you like to know?"

"Have you always been able to communicate with the dead?"

"Pretty much. As a kid I wasn't really sure what was going on at first, but my grandmother, who also had the gift, sat me down one day and explained it all. I was pretty arrogant back then and tried to dismiss it all. I'm ashamed to admit that I didn't pay a lot of attention to what she was telling me."

"I can't imagine what that must have been like." Beck sounded sincere. "Frankly, I haven't given much thought to that kind of thing. Val has tried to convince me that all this paranormal stuff is real, but I'm still having a difficult time accepting it all."

"I understand. It's not easy for some people to accept, but I can assure you, it's all very real," I told him. "And believe me, growing up with this gift was not fun."

"I can't begin to understand what you've gone through."

"Let's just say the kids in my neighborhood didn't want to hang around with someone who talked to people who weren't there."

"I'm sorry," Beck said quietly.

"Not your fault. And I survived." I chuckled humorlessly. I'd long since buried the hate, and I never wanted pity for what I'd gone through. "I didn't mean to be such a downer. Was there anything else you wanted to know?"

# fifteen

BECK

I FELT bad that I'd brought up such memories for Travis, but he didn't seem the type to want pity, so I moved on. "No more questions from me. But we're meeting because you wanted to know more about Kar. Is there anything specific you have in mind?"

"Nothing specific, I'm just trying to get a sense of who he was."

The server brought our food—a club sandwich for me and a roast beef on rye for Travis—and we continued our conversation as we ate. I relayed the story of how Kar and I met and shared stories from various times in our life. They were things I didn't often talk about with others. Val knew all of it, of course, but for some reason, I felt quite comfortable with Travis and was willing to talk about these things.

"Most of all," I neared the end of my discourse. "Kar was

kind. He cared about people, and that endeared him to me the most."

"Thank you," Travis said. "This helps a lot."

"Is there anything else you want to know about him?"

"No, I think I've learned all I need to. Kar loved you very much," Travis told me. "And even in death, it's clear that he still cares for you. I suspect that's why he hasn't fully moved on yet."

"What do you mean?" *Was he saying that Kar was roaming around because he still loved me?*

"I think Kar still feels some responsibility for you. Hopefully, the next time I encounter him, I can find out more."

Our conversation stalled a bit as we finished eating while I pondered everything Travis had said.

As we left the restaurant, Travis turned to me and said, "I appreciate the fact that you took the time to see me today. Not only did I learn some things about Kar that may help us, but I also enjoyed our time together."

It may have been my imagination, but Travis seemed to blush as he spoke those words. "I enjoyed myself too," I admitted. "Aside from Val, I don't go out very much anymore."

"I'm glad I was able to help. And please remember to let me know the next time something happens. No matter the time of day."

———

I WAS DISTRACTED all day Monday at work. I kept thinking about lunch with Travis the previous day. Something had stirred inside me during that meal. Something I hadn't felt in a long time and wasn't sure I was ready to admit to. I still loved Kar, so how could I feel something for someone else?

And the worse part of it all was that Val was still away, so I couldn't talk to her about it. At lunchtime, I sent a text, inviting her for dinner the following evening. That seemed to settle my brain a bit ,and I managed to get through the rest of the day.

After a dinner of leftover beef stew, I prepared a cottage pie for the next night's meal. But part of me was still thinking about Travis. Something in his manner the day before made the whole meeting feel almost like a date, but I couldn't put my finger on exactly why I felt that way. Just out of practice, I guess.

I slept fitfully that night, tossing and turning and dreaming of both Kar and Travis. In the dream, I was in bed with Kar, making love ...

*He traveled down my chest, slowly kissing and nibbling along the way until he reached my hard cock. Wrapping his lips around the head of my rigid shaft, he sucked me to the back of his throat.*

*"Mmm." I panted. Kar loved oral sex, and I loved how it felt to have his hot mouth surround me. "Coming!" I shouted, watching Kar swallow it all, then lick the head of my cock completely clean.*

*But when he looked up at me, it was Travis, not Kar that I saw.*

I woke up suddenly and realized that my shorts were damp with release. *What the hell?*

———

"Good morning, Val." I desperately tried to sound more cheerful than I felt. "Welcome back. I missed you."

"I missed you too, even though I had a wonderful time

with my sisters." She hugged me tightly in the parking lot of the pharmacy. "What's wrong?"

*Dammit, she could always see right through me!* "Nothing that can't wait until dinner tonight. I don't really want to get into it now."

She gave me a look that said she wasn't pleased with my decision, but she didn't push. Work kept us busy the entire day, but it didn't stop Val from giving me pointed looks every so often. When we got home, I put the cottage pie in the oven to heat.

As I opened a bottle of Root 1 Carmenere, Val said, "Okay, I know something's up, so just tell me now."

I poured her a glass of the wine and said, "I had lunch with Travis on Sunday."

"What? Why? Did Kar show himself in some way?" she asked.

"No, I haven't seen any evidence of Kar for a while. Travis called me on Saturday and said he wanted to get a little more background on Kar and suggested lunch."

"Okay," she said slowly. "But there's something else. Now spill."

"You're gonna think I'm crazy, but something about lunch almost felt like a date to me."

"A date? Really. In what way?" Val kept her tone even, but I could tell that this almost excited her.

"That's just it, I can't really explain it," I admitted. "Look, the fact of the matter is that I think I'm actually feeling something for Travis. It's, um, well, it's confusing because I haven't felt anything like this since Kar." I looked at her. "Am I crazy?"

"No, Beck, I don't think you're crazy at all. In fact, I think this is wonderful!" she exclaimed. "Frankly, it's about time you found someone you were interested in."

"But I still love Kar. And if he's really still here, isn't it wrong for me to be interested in someone else?"

"I don't really know. Maybe it's something that you need to talk to Kar about. I mean, Travis would be the perfect person to help you do that, right?"

"But what if I misread Sunday, and it's all just in my head? If Travis isn't interested in me, then this is gonna be really awkward."

"That's a valid point, but your gut doesn't usually mislead you, so I don't think you're misreading what happened," Val spoke sincerely. "Did he seem to be enjoying himself?"

"Yes, we both said that we had a nice time together." I'd decided that there was no way I was telling Val about the weird sex dream I had that involved both Kar *and* Travis.

"Perfect." Her eyes lit up. "I think you should call him tomorrow and maybe invite him over for dinner or something. And who knows, maybe Kar will take the hint and show up when the two of you are together."

Later that night, as I prepared for bed, I thought about what Val had said. I didn't completely understand the feelings I was having, but one thing I knew for certain was that I wanted to see Travis again. Maybe inviting him over for dinner was exactly what I needed to do.

# sixteen

TRAVIS

I SPENT Wednesday morning dealing with a stubborn spirit who refused to move on. They were also hesitant to tell me why. When I finally left, just after lunchtime, I'd secured a promise from the entity, whose name was George, that he'd tell me more when I returned in a couple of days. Sometimes that was the way with spirits—it took a while to convince them that it was time to move on.

Thanks to some of the techniques that Auntie Mae had shown me—I'd met with her a few more times and had learned so much more—I wasn't completely exhausted when I got home, but after a quick lunch, I decided to take a little nap anyway.

I woke a couple of hours later to my phone ringing.

"Hello," I answered, not bothering to look at the screen.

"Hi, Travis, it's Beck."

"Hey, Beck. Is everything okay? Did something happen in the house that you think might be Kar?"

"No, not yet. I just got home from work and was thinking about our lunch on Sunday. I had a really good time, and I was wondering if you'd be interested in getting together again. Maybe you could come over for dinner on Saturday?"

"You mean like a date?"

"Let's just say two friends getting together for dinner."

"I'd like that, Beck. Thanks." There was a smile in my voice.

"Great. How about seven o'clock?"

"That works. Can I bring anything?"

"I haven't decided what I'll make yet. Is there anything you're allergic to or something that you don't like?"

"I'm not fussy at all, and no, not allergic to any foods," I told him.

"How about pasta? I've got some homemade Bolognese in the freezer."

"Perfect. I'll pick up some red wine." The liquor store nearby had a decent selection of non-alcoholic wines; there was no reason I couldn't pick up a bottle of that for me along with something nice for Beck.

We rang off, and I suddenly had the feeling that I wasn't alone in my home. Remembering my training, I quickly grounded and centered myself and stretched out my senses, trying to get a feel for who might be there.

"Who's here?" I called out. "I know someone's here."

*It's me, Karson,* a voice popped into my head, and slowly, the spirit of Kar appeared before me. He was tall and had a kind face framed by a mane of white locks, but worry clouded his eyes. After a few seconds, he vanished, but his presence still lingered.

"Karson? What are you doing here?"

*I wanted to talk to you. Alone. I figured the best way would be to come here. I hope that's okay.*

"Of course," I replied, still a bit shocked that he had come here to speak to me. "What is it that you wanted to talk to me about?" I'd spoken telepathically with Auntie Mae a few more times since our first meeting, but I still felt more comfortable speaking aloud to the dead.

*It's about Beck. I'm worried about him.*

"What do you mean, worried? Is something wrong?" I sensed he was holding back something. "What aren't you telling me?"

*Oh, you're good, Travis. From what I've been told, not many among the living can see and hear us, let alone sense our moods and feelings.*

"I've been seeing and hearing spirits since I was a kid. I've gotten better about discerning things regarding them as I get older."

*I've spent almost five years wandering around, feeling like I needed to do something before I moved on. I think I may have finally figured it out.*

"Okay. Is that why you've suddenly decided to make yourself known to Beck? Because you'll be moving on and won't be checking in on him anymore?"

*That's part of it. I think Beck is the reason I haven't moved on yet. You see, he hasn't really moved on yet either. In so many ways, he's still grieving my death. He needs to realize that he's got so much to live for. I think I'm still here so that I can help him find love again.*

"Okay." I wasn't sure exactly where Kar was going with this. "Why are you telling me this? I'm not sure if Beck would listen to anything *I* would say to him. After all, he's still not fully convinced that you're really here."

*Travis, I think you're the one.*

"I'm the one what? What are you talking about?"

*I think you and Beck belong together. I can't explain it, but I feel something, some connection between the two of you.*

"Really? That's interesting." I wasn't sure if I should say anything more but quickly decided that I had nothing to lose. "The fact is, I do think about Beck quite a bit. You're right, I do feel some kind of connection to him, but I thought it was my imagination. It's been too long since I was attracted to anyone."

*I believe you need to tell him how you feel.*

"Are you serious? How in the hell do I say anything to him without sounding like a creep who's trying to take advantage of the situation?"

*Hmmm, you're right. That does sound rather creepy, doesn't it? I think first we need to get him to believe that it's really me. Once he believes it's me, I can try to convince him that he needs someone like you in his life.*

"Okay. Do you have any idea about how we can make him believe?"

*I do. It's clear to me at this point that the physical manifestations are just confusing him. I'd hoped that they would convince him it was me, but apparently my husband is more stubborn than I remember.* I heard a distinct chuckle in Kar's voice. *There's actually a nickname I used to call Beck that I'm ninety-nine percent sure he never told anyone. Not even Val.*

"Okay. That could definitely work," I said. "Oh, wait, I just had a thought. Beck just called me and invited me over for dinner Saturday night. Maybe you could show up while I'm there. I can be the conduit so you can talk to him."

*Beck called you? Hmmm, maybe this won't be as difficult as I thought.*

"Whoa. Slow down there, Karson. He just said it was two friends having dinner. But who knows? I've been told I can be quite charming when I want to be."

Kar's laugh in response was not as comforting as I'd hoped.

———

ON SATURDAY EVENING, I arrived at Beck's house and sat in the driveway for a moment. I still wasn't exactly sure why Beck had invited me over for dinner, and that caused a few butterflies in my stomach. I hadn't dated anyone in quite a while, and the thought of spending time with Beck in a purely social situation was a bit unsettling. For good measure, I took a moment to ground and center myself, then grabbed the wine I'd picked up and walked to the front door.

"Hi, Travis," Beck greeted me. He led me to the kitchen, where there was a charcuterie board set up on the island. "I thought we could snack on this while I finish up dinner prep. Can I get you something to drink?"

"Did you want to open the wine now?" I asked.

"Let's save that for dinner. I was gonna pour myself a bourbon on the rocks."

"Just some water for me, thanks. Sparkling if you have it." I sat at the island and munched on a piece of cheese while Beck chopped vegetables for a salad.

"This will just take me a few minutes. Did you want to eat right away or relax a little first?"

"Normally, I'd say relax a little, but frankly, I'm kind of hungry," I admitted. "I got caught up in a project at home and skipped lunch."

"No problem. I already heated up the Bolognese, and it's keeping warm on the stove, so I'll just start the water for the pasta now," Beck told me.

I watched him chop celery and peppers and skillfully dice tomatoes. "You're awfully good at that," I commented, smiling. "I don't cook at home very much although I can cook a steak or a burger, and I make a mean grilled cheese."

Beck chuckled. "Well, you seem to have the basics down. I've always enjoyed cooking although when Kar was alive, he did most of it, at least during the week."

"Why was that?" I asked.

"He worked from home and would get started on the meal prep once he was done for the day. By the time I got home, dinner was ready. It became a comfortable routine for us, although I sometimes would prepare a meal on the weekend."

"That sounds nice."

"It was. Now I cook some of our favorite meals, kind of as a tribute to him. Funny, try as I might, I still remember his versions tasting so much better than mine."

"Really? Based on the delicious aromas coming from that pot of sauce, I find that hard to believe. Maybe I'll need to convince you to make some of those dishes for me so I can taste them for myself," I said, keeping my voice light. *Just a little flirting with Beck was okay, right?*

"I'd like that."

# seventeen

BECK

I FINISHED the salad and set it on the small table in front of the bank of windows at the end of the kitchen. I'd set the table earlier, so everything was ready to go. While the spaghetti cooked, I sat at the island and sipped my drink as we made small talk about our lives.

"So, it sounds like you and Val go way back. You met in college, right?"

"Yeah. She's been a great friend for many years. I feel very fortunate to have her in my life. In many ways she's the sister I never had," I said. "Do you have anyone like that in your life?"

"I do," Travis replied honestly. "Tony—he owns the Raven's Claw—and I have been friends for a long time. In fact, he's probably my only real friend. In many ways, he's like family too. We've been through a lot together, and I know he'll always have my back."

"That's good. Sometimes the family we choose can be so much better than those we're related to by blood."

The timer rang, and I rose to check the pasta. I quickly drained it, saving some of the liquid, and tossed it with some of the Bolognese. It had thickened while keeping warm, so I used the pasta water to thin it out a bit, then filled two bowls with the steaming food.

As Travis opened the wine, I nodded toward the bottles and said, "I'm curious. Why do you have two different bottles of wine?"

"Ah. Well, the truth is, I try not to drink alcohol very much. Over the years, when the spirits get a bit too talkative, I've used my buddy Jack Daniels to help drown out the noise." Travis turned away slightly, as if embarrassed by the admission. "I still enjoy a drink occasionally but try not to overdo it as much anymore."

"Hey. No worries." I kept my tone soothing. "I'm sorry I brought it up."

"It's fine," he replied, clearly trying to force a smile. "So I picked up this bottle of non-alcoholic red to try. The guy at the liquor store said it was quite popular." He poured a glass from each bottle, and we sat to enjoy our repast.

———

"OH MY GOD, THAT WAS FANTASTIC!" Travis patted his stomach.

"I'm glad you enjoyed it." Against my protests, he helped me load the dishwasher and tidy up the kitchen.

When we were finished, I turned to him. "Why don't we relax in the den?" There was still some wine in each of the bottles. "If you grab the bottles, I'll carry in the wine glasses."

He sat at one end of the overstuffed couch, and I took the matching club chair on the right.

"I was kind of surprised when you invited me to dinner tonight," Travis said.

"Really? We both had a good time at lunch on Sunday, so to me it seemed natural for us to get together again."

"I agree lunch was fun, but as I said on the phone when you called me, this kinda feels like a date. Am I wrong?"

"Honestly, I'm not sure." I willed my voice to remain steady. "I don't know if I should admit this, but since the first time we met, I felt … something. Um, like a connection or, I dunno. Something. But it scares me." I spoke quietly, afraid to even look at Travis.

"Why does it scare you?"

"Because I really haven't felt anything like this since Kar. I miss him, and I still love him so much. Somehow this feels wrong. I shouldn't have feelings for someone else."

I turned to Travis and saw he had a strange look on his face as if he were staring into nothingness.

"What's wrong?"

"I think Kar is here. I just felt something." He paused for a moment, then said, "Karson, is that you?" He hesitated as if listening to someone.

"Kar *is* here," he told me. "He says that he heard what you said, and he still loves you too, but it's okay if you develop feelings for another person."

"Really?" I couldn't keep the skepticism from my voice. "I'm supposed to believe that Kar chose this moment to show up and tell me that it's okay to feel something for you? Isn't that rather convenient?" I sipped my wine, trying to calm my sudden nervousness.

"Oh, Toddy," Travis said, "I forgot how stubborn you can be. It's really me standing here. Maybe this will convince you."

And with that, one of the desk drawers slowly slid open, and something rose out as if supported by an invisible hand, landing on the desk.

"What?" I stared at Travis in disbelief. "What did you call me?"

"Um, Toddy. But I don't know what that means. Kar just told me to say that exactly as he said it to me. Does it mean something?"

"It's a nickname that Kar had for me. Oh God." I rubbed the back of my neck, shaking my head. "This can't be happening." I closed my eyes and breathed for a moment. I went to the desk and saw Kar's old driver's license sitting there once again. I looked back at Travis and quietly asked, "Is he really here?" At Travis's nod, I continued, my voice quivering, "Ask him why he called me that."

"He says that you two used to drink hot toddies made from warm apple cider, bourbon, and a splash of Fireball. One night he said that you were just like that drink—hot and sweet. And then he said he loved you and called you Toddy. Ever since, he's called you that nickname during sweet moments between the two of you."

I returned to my chair on unsteady feet, my hands shaking. I looked around the room, scanning for something, anything that might be Kar. "Is it really you, Kar? Are you really here?" I whispered.

"Kar says, 'Yes, Toddy,'" Travis said. "'I'm really here.'"

"Why did you wait so long to contact me?" I asked, feeling aggrieved. "I've missed you so much!"

After a few moments, Travis looked at me. "He says he knows, and he's sorry. At first he didn't really know that he'd be staying around this long and was afraid that if he tried to reach out and then left, it would be worse for you. Then he wasn't really sure why he wasn't moving on and spent some time talking with other spirits and figuring stuff out." Travis paused once again, staring off into space. "Kar believes he knows why he stayed this long and feels he may be moving on soon. This was his one last chance to contact you."

"What do you mean? Why did you stay, Kar?"

"Kar says he thinks he stayed to help you find love again. He thinks you have a chance now, so he'll probably be moving on to the next plane before too long." Travis paused as if listening once again. "Kar says he's going to do one last thing tonight, but it will exhaust most of his energy, and then he'll need to leave. But he'll come back again soon."

At that moment, I saw Kar, standing near the desk. He was mostly transparent, but I could clearly see his handsome face. He smiled. Then he was gone.

"Oh my God," I cried out. "Did you see that?"

Travis nodded slowly. "I did. It's very unusual for spirits to show themselves. It takes tremendous power on their part. I'm sure that's why he's gone now. To replenish himself."

We sat in silence for a while. I was rather unnerved and didn't quite know what to say. Finally, once I'd had time to process all that had happened, I looked at Travis and said, "Thank you so much for coming here tonight. Yes, I believe Kar was really here, but I do need some time to digest all of this. It might be normal for you, but I've never encountered anything like this before."

# eighteen



I DROVE HOME in somewhat of a daze that night. After Kar made his appearance, literally, Beck became quiet, though his mood didn't seem sad or depressed. I was glad that he admitted to believing that Kar was indeed still around, and I understood that he still needed some time to process everything. It somehow made him even more attractive to me. I left with a promise to call him the following day to check in on him.

What Kar had done was rather bold. First telling Beck that he had a chance to find love again, and then to actually show himself. I couldn't imagine what thoughts were racing through Beck's mind.

Did Kar really believe that Beck and I would end up together? Honestly, I wasn't opposed to it at all. I'd been intrigued by Beck since the first time I met him and would love to see if this led to something between us, but it wasn't entirely up to me. I only hoped that Kar's appearance this evening hadn't scared Beck.

All of these thoughts flowed through my mind as I got ready for bed, and I was fully aware that there was nothing I could do about it right now. My only hope was to try and relax, emptying my mind as I laid there, willing myself to sleep.

———

I WOKE to a gray and drizzly day. It somewhat matched my mood, but I told myself that wallowing wasn't helpful. I was standing in front of my refrigerator, staring at the nearly empty shelves while trying to figure out if there was something I could make for breakfast, when my phone rang.

"Hey, Tone," I answered, seeing my friend's name on the display.

"Good morning, Trav," Tony replied, a smile in his voice, knowing I hated that nickname. "Have you had breakfast yet?" he asked.

No," I replied. "I was just trying to figure out what I could make with half a carton of leftover chicken fried rice and a slice of what might be American cheese." I sighed. "Apparently, I haven't been food shopping in a while."

"Meet me at Sam's in twenty minutes," was his laughing reply. Sam's was a diner on the edge of town that we frequented.

He was sitting in a booth, sipping his black coffee, when I arrived. Sliding into the bench across from him, I watched as our waitress Janice sauntered over.

"Morning, Travis," she said, filling my cup. "The usual?" *See, I told you we came here often.*

"Yes, please," I replied. A Western omelet with home fries and whole wheat toast would hit the spot.

"So how was the date last night?" Tony asked.

"Ah, so that's why you invited me to breakfast this morning. And it wasn't a date."

"First of all, you have a track record for not grocery shopping regularly, so I figured you'd be up for a good meal, and second, I know you've got the hots for this new client, so I assumed that getting invited to his house for dinner would be a date-like evening. Was I wrong?"

"Let's just say it was an interesting evening."

"I take that to mean that you didn't get lucky?"

"Okay, that's crude even for you, Tony," I said. "And things kinda went south when his husband showed up."

"His dead husband? Wow. That's ... different. So like a ménage à ghost?"

"Stop it. But yeah, though it wasn't totally unexpected."

"Whaddya mean?" Tony's face scrunched up.

"I guess I should back up a bit. Kar came to see me the other day."

"Wait. The spirit of the dead husband visited you at your house? Why?"

"He wanted to talk to me without Beck there. He said he had finally figured out why he's been hanging around for five years and hasn't moved on yet." Our conversation stalled as Janice arrived with two heaping plates of food.

"Be right back with more coffee, fellas," she said as she hurried away.

"So what did Kar tell you?" Tony asked.

"He's of the opinion that Beck hasn't really moved on with his life, and Kar thinks he's still around to help Beck find love again. Once that happens, he feels it will be time to transition to the next plane.”

“Interesting.”

“There’s more,” I continued. “He thinks maybe I’m the person that can make Beck happy again.”

“Really? So he’s trying to fix up the two of you? Is that why he showed up at dinner last night? Imagine, a matchmaking ghost! This is crazy!” Tony’s voice slowly rose in pitch.

“Mostly, he showed up last night to try and convince Beck that he’s real. And I think he finally succeeded. He called Beck a nickname that he used to use and took his old driver’s license out of the desk drawer. Finally, he did something really amazing.”

“More amazing than manipulating real objects? What did he do?”

“He appeared so that Beck could actually see him.”

“Seriously? Granted, I can’t do the things that you do, but I’ve got enough of the gift that I understand how much energy that took, especially after the other stuff he did.”

“I know. He was visible for only a handful of seconds, smiled at Beck, and then disappeared. Beck got kind of quiet after that.”

“I can’t imagine what was going through Beck’s head after all that,” Tony said.

“I know. I thought the same thing. I promised to call him today to check on him. I’ll do that when I get home.”

“Sorry I teased you about getting lucky,” Tony said quietly. “I didn’t realize what was going on.”

“No worries,” I told my friend. “It’s not what I expected at all when I took on this case, but if I’m totally honest, I’m not really opposed to it,” I admitted. “I don’t know what it is, but there’s something extremely fascinating about Beckett Gray.”

"But this has to be really difficult for him."

"Right? Hopefully he'll talk to me later."

We finished our meal in companionable silence.

———

As soon as I got home, I called Beck. He answered almost immediately.

"How are you doing?" I asked softly.

"Okay, I guess. What happened last night is just a lot to process."

"Did you get much sleep, or did you lie awake, thinking about it all?"

"I did sleep some, but yeah, I also did my fair share of just lying there thinking about everything." He sighed quietly.

"Don't beat yourself up over that, Beck," I told him. "It's only natural. After all, that was a lot to absorb all at once."

"Yeah, I guess. I need to think about this a little more."

"And if I've learned anything at all about you, I'm guessing you need to talk to Val, right?"

Beck chuckled. "You're absolutely right." He paused, but I sensed he had more to say, so I kept silent. "All I ask," he finally said, "is that you're patient with me. I need a little time to sort out all these feelings."

"I understand," I said sincerely. "And remember, I'm here if you need to talk."

"Thanks, Travis. I appreciate that. I'll call you in a couple of days."

We ended the call, and I sat there for a moment. A feeling of peace settled around me, as I knew that even though it might take a while, everything was gonna be okay.

# nineteen

BECK

I was as honest as I could be with Travis. Last night had really shaken me. But yes, I now knew that Kar's spirit was indeed still around, and if he was to be believed, watching over me to a degree. That in itself felt a little creepy, but he was, after all, my husband, so it didn't freak me out too much.

But I was rather shocked when he said that he thought perhaps there could be something between Travis and me. Sure, I felt something between us, but I wasn't exactly sure what it was. Could Kar be somehow manipulating me? Was that possible? *Argh, this is just too confusing!*

Travis was right, though. This was something I needed to talk to Val about. I'd texted her early this morning to beg off our normal Sunday brunch together, weakly saying that I hadn't slept well and would explain it all later. Thankfully, she didn't push me at that point, but after talking with Travis, I was prepared now.

"Are you ready to tell me what's *really* going on?" she asked by way of greeting when I called.

"Yeah," I said sheepishly. "I'm sorry, but I needed to think through a few things."

"Did something happen last night at dinner with Travis? If he hurt you, I'll kill him, and I promise you, they'll never find the body."

"Oh, Val." I laughed heartily. "Never change, please."

"Hey," she replied, "you're family, and nobody fucks with my family."

"First of all, Travis didn't hurt me. Second, I love you, don't ever forget that. I want to tell you everything—"

"Of course, you do," she interrupted.

"But we're gonna need alcohol. Can you come over?"

"Of course. And I'll bring a change of clothes. If we're gonna start drinking this early, I'll probably need to stay over."

"Good idea. See you in a little while." Less than an hour later, I heard Val's car pull into the driveway.

As we hugged at the door, Val asked, "Are you okay?"

"I will be," I replied honestly. "There's wine, but I'm having bourbon." I retreated to the den, letting Val fend for herself. After all, she'd spent enough time here that she knew where everything was.

Val joined me a couple of minutes later with an ice-filled glass. "I figured I'd start with bourbon as well. I can always move to wine later." She smirked.

I raised my glass as she poured a healthy measure into her own. "Cheers."

"So tell me what happened."

I recounted my dinner with Travis the previous evening. "It started off rather well. We had Bolognese with a salad and some wine. We chatted about everyday stuff. After dinner, we cleaned up together, and it felt very domestic. Then we sat in here, and I admitted that I felt something for him, but that it scared me a little since I hadn't really felt like that for anyone since Kar."

"Okay. Does he not feel the same way?"

"I really don't know. Right after I told him, he got this faraway look in his eyes and then said that Kar was here."

"What?"

I sipped at my bourbon. "Right?" I shook my head. "And then he called me Toddy. It was … I dunno, surreal, I guess."

"Whaddya mean he called you Toddy? Why would Travis call you Toddy? I don't understand."

"Not Travis, Kar. Toddy was a silly nickname Kar had for me. Didn't I ever tell …" I trailed off, thinking hard. "No, I guess I never did." I explained the nickname, and she stared at me.

"So that's when you knew that Kar was really here."

"Well, that was only the beginning. He then took his driver's license out of the desk drawer where I keep it, and then … oh God, and then I saw him!"

"You saw Kar?" Her voice was incredulous.

"Yeah. He was standing right there." I pointed to the edge of the desk. "He smiled at me, then he was gone."

"Oh, Beck!"

"I guess I need to apologize to you, Val."

"Apologize? Why?"

"Because I never really believed in ghosts and the supernatural, as hard as you tried to convince me. But I was wrong. It's all very real."

"Hell of a way to find out, though," she said softly.

"Yeah. Well. It is what it is. And, well, there's more."

"There's more?"

"It seems that Kar feels that he's been hanging around—I'm not sure what else to call it— but he's still here because he's been waiting for me to find love again, and he thinks Travis may be the answer."

"So he's playing matchmaker from the beyond?"

"I guess. And that's one of the things I'm really having a problem with."

"Why? You did say that you feel something there, right?"

"Yeah, but I also kinda feel like I'm being manipulated. I dunno. Somehow this all feels too convenient."

"I can see how you'd feel that way, but I've never heard of any instance where a spirit was able to control someone like that. Oh, I suppose there are truly evil people who stay evil when they die, but Kar wasn't like that, Beck. You know that."

"Yeah, but—"

"But nothing," Val cut me off. "You've had physical evidence of Kar's presence, and while I don't know much about Travis, I can tell you that I do trust Tony; I've never known him to be anything less than honorable. I can't imagine that he'd recommend someone like Travis if he wasn't a good guy too." I could hear the sincerity in Val's voice, and it bolstered me.

"You're right, I'm just being a whiny bitch." I attempted a smile. "Okay, the question that needs asking is, what do I do now?"

"If you really do feel something for Travis, I think you should pursue it. But slowly," she cautioned. "If Kar is really okay with this, and something in my gut says that he is, then I don't really believe you're in any danger, but take your time. Get to know Travis better and see what happens. Trust your heart."

"Thanks, sweetie," I said, smiling. "Now let's see what I can rustle up for dinner."

———

I WAS LYING in bed that night, going over my conversation with Val. As it turned out, we didn't really have all that much to drink, and Val went home around nine, leaving me to my thoughts.

I was finally comfortable with the fact that Kar's spirit was really still around, and the more I thought about it, the less scary it seemed. It was actually quite reassuring that he was keeping an eye on me. And Val was right, he wouldn't do anything to hurt me.

As for Travis, yes, I wanted to know more about him. If I was gonna be completely honest with myself, I wanted to go out on a real and proper date with him. Flirt a bit, even. God, it had been so long, and I was sorely out of practice, but something deep inside me wanted this. I'd take Val's advice and go slowly, though. There was no reason to rush into anything.

I drifted off to sleep thinking about Travis and his sweet smile and kind eyes.

# twenty

KAR

I woke to find myself lying in the grass near the side garden of what used to be my house. Well, "woke" wasn't really the right word, as I hadn't actually been asleep.

Materializing in front of Beck had taken quite a bit of energy, and I'd already used up some to take my license out of the desk drawer, so I retreated to the lawn near the garden to rest up and rebuild my reserves. I stayed there in a state of rest, fully aware of my surroundings but not really able to do much. I felt quite drained but knew from past experiences that it was only a matter of time before I'd be back to my old self. I'd closed my eyes and feigned sleep, making it feel more normal for me to just lie there and rest.

When I finally felt more like myself, I rose and transported myself to the park bench where I often saw Joseph. It wasn't long before he came strolling by and sat beside me.

"I haven't seen you for a little while. How are things, Kar?" he asked.

"Okay, I guess. I did something, I think it was yesterday. I overdid it and have been resting. It may have been the day before."

"This sounds serious." Joseph was solemn. "What did you do?"

"I went to see Beck. He was having dinner with the medium I told you about. I told Travis to call Beck by a nickname I used to use, and then I, um, well, I showed myself to him."

"I see. And how did he react to all that?"

"I think he finally believes that I'm here. I mean, I was at a loss for what else to do. I *had* to make him believe. I just hope I didn't make things worse."

"I don't understand. Why wouldn't this be a good thing? You wanted Beck to believe you are really here."

"Well, I may have alluded to the fact that I think Travis could be the one to help him find love again."

"Ah. Now it makes sense." Joseph nodded slowly.

"And because I overdid it, I disappeared shortly after I materialized, so I'm not sure how Beck is feeling about everything right now."

"Well, Kar, I think you need to go back and check."

"I'm scared."

"Be that as it may, you need to know. But something tells me that everything will be all right. From what you've told me about Beck, he seems to be a rational man."

"I hope you're right, Joseph. Thank you for listening. I believe I'll just sit for a little while longer and then check on him."

———

I approached the house slowly, enjoying the view of the pale-sage clapboard and the oak front door. I was happy that Beck had hired someone to keep up the gardens that I loved so much. He always joked that he could kill a silk ivy, but he knew how much the yard meant to me. *Ah, well, enough woolgathering.*

There was no car in the driveway, so I guessed it was a weekday, and Beck wasn't home from work yet. I ambled along to the back door and entered the kitchen, wondering if I'd need to wait long before my love got home. Glancing around, perhaps for the first time since I'd passed, I noticed a few changes here and there, but it was pretty much as I remembered it. I chuckled to myself. It was so like Beck to keep things as they were; he wasn't really a fan of change. Which was probably why he'd yet to move on with his life.

Just then, I heard some noise outside, and a few moments later, Beck walked in the front door. He hung his jacket on the coat-tree and slogged down the hall, the weight of the world seeming to rest on his shoulders.

"Why were you taken from me, Kar?" he suddenly cried out.

*I'm here, sweetheart.* It pained me that he couldn't hear my response, couldn't feel my presence. I was overwhelmed with emotion and couldn't bear to see him in such agony. This was too much. I willed myself to the park, hoping for some solace in the trees.

———

**BECK**

. . .

WHEN I GOT HOME Monday evening after work, I almost hoped I'd see some sign of Kar's presence. But no muddy boot prints, no flowers. Nothing.

Shedding my coat, I plodded to the den and flung myself into my recliner. "Why were you taken from me, Kar?" I cried out. "I bitched at you so many times for leaving those muddy prints on the front porch, but I'd give anything to see them again. To see you again." A sob caught in my throat.

I shook my head, feeling a bit foolish about my outburst. I didn't even know if Kar could hear me. He probably wasn't there. But I waited, hoping beyond hope that somehow he knew how much I wanted to see him.

Sighing, I stood and turned toward the kitchen. I didn't have much of an appetite but still needed to eat, so I went in search of nourishment.

# twenty-one

BECK

THE WEEK DRAGGED ON. I'd spent much of my free time going over everything that had occurred. There were chats with Val, much soul searching, and that incident earlier in the week with Kar.

The reality that I'd come to accept was that Kar was indeed still around. And he was, after being dead for almost five years, trying to make himself known to me because he thought I needed to find love again so that he could move on. Yeah, it felt surreal most of the time, but who was I to argue at this point?

I'd also sort of accepted the fact that there might actually be something between Travis and me. I had definitely felt some attraction to him even before Kar tried to push us together. I decided that the next step was finding out how Travis felt about all of this. So on Thursday evening, I picked up the phone.

"Hi, Beck," he answered.

"Hey, Travis, how's it going?" I hoped I sounded calmer than I felt.

"Okay. Did something happen? Has Kar tried to contact you again?"

"No, that's not why I'm calling right now. Do you have time to chat?"

"Sure," Travis said. "What's going on?"

"Well, I guess I wanna know what happens now?"

"What do you mean?" Travis sounded confused.

"Sorry," I said. "My bad. I kinda just jumped right into the middle, didn't I? Everything's been spinning around in my head. Let me explain." I took a deep breath along with a sip of the bourbon I'd poured for myself before placing the call. "I can't deny it anymore. Kar is really here. Well, his spirit is anyway. But I mean with us. I sort of admitted to you the other night that I do feel something between us, but after Kar showed up I ... well, I don't want to feel manipulated here. Kar seems to fancy himself to be a matchmaker of sorts, and I don't know how I feel about that. Not to mention the fact that I'm not entirely sure what you think about it all. I'm sorry if I'm rambling, but I guess what I'm asking is, how do *you* feel about all of this?"

I was met by silence on the other end of the line, and my heart sank. I should never have called him.

Finally, after several moments, Travis began to speak. "Well, the truth is, I also felt something between us. From the first time we met, actually. When we shook hands in your foyer that first day, I felt a spark or something when we touched. I wasn't exactly sure what it was. It happened again when we met for lunch," he said quietly. "And if I'm being completely honest, that's never happened to me before. But if you're interested, I'd like to see where this leads. Between us, I mean."

"I'd like that too," I admitted. "Would you consider going out with me? Perhaps for dinner Saturday night?" While it was true that Val and I often got together on Saturday evenings, she would completely understand if I missed one of our card games for this.

"I'd like that a lot," Travis replied.

"Great. Text me your address, and I'll pick you up at seven."

"See you then."

———

I'D DECIDED on Fiddler's for our dinner on Saturday. It was casual, and I felt comfortable there, so I hoped it would help ease my nerves a bit.

I dressed in dark jeans with a burgundy thermal Henley over a white T-shirt. That, paired with my favorite green barn jacket, completed my outfit. Kar had bought me the jacket shortly before he died. I'd seen it in an L.L.Bean catalog but hadn't wanted to spend the money, so Kar had surprised me with it for no other reason than he wanted me to be happy.

I was a few minutes early, but Travis must have seen me pull up since he immediately walked out of his house and got into my car.

Travis looked amazing. He wore a black button-down paired with black jeans and the ever-present crystals around his neck, topped off by his leather jacket. Truth be told, I was having difficulty breathing just from looking at him.

While I don't normally make a reservation at Fiddler's, I had done so this time because it was a Saturday, and I was taking no chances. We were immediately led to a back booth. As we walked past the bar, Dennis nodded at me, a questioning look on his face. I almost exclusively sat at the bar, so I was sure he was wondering what was going on.

"So," I said after we were settled and had ordered drinks, "tell me about those stones you wear around your neck."

He fingered the items slung together on a black leather cord. "This one," he said, stopping to run the pad of his thumb along a black faceted crystal, "is black tourmaline. My grandmother gave it to me when I was just a kid. She told me that many consider it to be the king of protective crystals, and I should never take it off. Supposedly, it can also change negative energy into positive energy." He spoke reverently when he mentioned his grandmother.

"I'm guessing by your tone that you don't ever take it off?"

"Never. All of these stones are special, and each of them are meant to assist with protection. They were all given to me and mean something in my life. I didn't pay enough attention to what Grandma tried to tell me for so long, but I figured I should listen to her about this. The one next to it"—his fingers traveled to a whitish stone—"is clear quartz. It's a healing stone and can amplify properties like the energy or protection of other stones. Tony gave it to me shortly after we met.

"This brown stone"—he moved to the polished one next—"is tiger's-eye. It also offers protection and boosts the confidence and courage of its wearer. A client gave it to me in lieu of payment a few years ago."

I marveled at his knowledge of these things. Now that I was more receptive to these paranormal elements, I considered asking him for advice about getting my own to wear. "I have to tell you, I'm intrigued by all of this. Please tell me more."

His fingers deftly moved to the next stone—a smooth and iridescent beauty. "This is labradorite. It was also a gift from Tony, quite recently, in fact. It's supposed to enhance psychic abilities and also protects against negative energy." He smiled wistfully and sipped his non-alcoholic beer. "There's actually a story behind this one. For quite a while, Tony had been trying to convince me to meet with a friend of his named Auntie Mae. She has the gift as well, and Tony thought she might be able to help me since I never really got any formal training when I was younger. Anyway, when I finally agreed, he pulled this out of his pocket and handed it to me. Which leads me to this last item." He stroked the next stone, shiny and black.

"This is hematite. It not only offers protection but helps wearers ground and center themselves. That's critical, as I recently learned, when working with psychic energy and dealing with spirits. Auntie Mae gave it to me."

"I sense there's more to this story. You'll need to tell me about this grounding and centering, but maybe we should think about ordering some food."

"You're right." He chuckled, and I realized how much I loved the sound of his laughter. "What's good here?" he asked, scanning the menu, which I knew by heart.

I offered a few recommendations, then caught the eye of our server and we ordered—a spicy chicken sandwich for me and a patty melt for Travis.

# twenty-two

TRAVIS

"Now, I've been bending your ear about my trinkets long enough," I said. "Let's talk about you for a while."

"What do you want to know?" Beck asked.

"Well, let's see. ... I know you're a pharmacist and that you spend a fair amount of time with Val, but I don't really know much else about you. Do you have any hobbies?"

"I do, actually," he replied. He seemed hesitant, almost embarrassed to say more. "I write a bit."

"Write? Like books?"

"Well, no actual book yet, but I've had a few short stories published, yeah."

"That's very cool. I must admit, I don't read a lot, but I'd like to read something that you've written," I said.

"I have some extra copies of the literary magazine they were published in," Beck told me. "I'll give you a copy."

"Thanks. So you said no book yet. Does that mean you're actually working on a book?" My curiosity was getting the better of me.

"I am." Beck paused, sipping at his sauvignon blanc. "Frankly, a lot of what I've written—or tried to write—in the past often dealt with death and could get rather depressing. But I'm trying something new. A romance. Specifically, a gay romance. No death, no dying, just some love and happiness."

"I think that sounds great. When you finish—that's right, I said *when* because I believe you're gonna do this—can I have an autographed copy?"

"Of course." A smile appeared on his face, and it was as if the sun had just broken through a cluster of clouds. Beck was radiant, and I once again realized how much I was growing to care about this man.

"So," I continued, "when I visited your home, I saw the beautiful flower beds all around. Is that your doing?"

He barked a laugh. "Not at all. Kar said I had a black thumb and could probably kill silk plants. He was the gardener in the family. As a tribute to him, I continue to maintain them, thanks to a local gardening and landscaping service," he finished quietly.

"I'm sorry if I brought up something painful to you."

"No worries. I don't mind talking about it now. When Kar first passed, it was quite painful. I couldn't bear to even *look* at the flowers in the yard for the longest time. Everything became overgrown, and that only made me feel worse since Kar had loved it all so much."

"I can't imagine what you went through."

"If not for Val, I think I could have gone over the edge at that point. She was always there, helping me through it all."

"You're very lucky to have her."

"I know, but please don't tell her that." Beck grinned wickedly. "She already thinks too much of herself. Can't have her lording it over me more than she already does."

"Your secret's safe with me." I smiled, and I felt something change between us. A deepening of ... I wasn't sure what, but yeah, something happened just then.

Our food arrived, and we dug in, moving on to lighter topics like movies and TV shows that we enjoyed.

We were quiet on our way home, seemingly talked out. When we arrived at my home, Beck put the vehicle in park and turned. His face was partly hidden in shadow, a result of the dim streetlamp just down the block.

"I really enjoyed myself tonight," he told me. "I'd like to see you again if that's okay."

"I'd like that," I replied. "I'm not much of a cook, but there are a few things I learned from my grandma. Perhaps you'd like to come over next week?"

"That would be nice. Call me so we can finalize the details."

I leaned over and kissed Beck chastely on the lips. "I'll do that. And thanks again for dinner."

———

BECK

LATER THAT EVENING, as I lay in bed, my thoughts again turned to Travis. Even after what had been a painful admission for him when he spoke about how he generally refrains from consuming alcohol, we had enjoyed a pleasant dinner together. At least, I had. And based on the fact that Travis kissed me, I thought he'd enjoyed himself as well.

What was it about this man that I found so fascinating? Sure, he was handsome, with his dark hair and warm brown eyes that seemed to look into your very soul. But there was something more. Part of him seemed tortured. That might be due to the issues he's had with alcohol; I hoped it wasn't anything more than that. But beyond all of that, there was a kindness about this man. The desire to help that seemed to break through, no matter the cost to him.

———

MORNING DAWNED BRIGHT AND COOL, a perfect fall day. I sat in my recliner and stared out into the backyard, sipping my coffee and thinking again about my date with Travis. Of course, I'd tell Val all about it over brunch. I was, in fact, surprised that she hadn't called to ask about it already. She was certainly showing some restraint. Fortified with the much-needed caffeine, I hurried upstairs to get ready to meet Val.

While I was dressing, my phone buzzed—a text from Travis that put a smile on my face.

**I had a great time last night. And I meant it when I said I wanted you to come over this week. Would Thursday night work for you?**

———

VAL and I both pulled into the restaurant's parking lot at the same time, and she hurried over, giving me a warm hug and kissing my cheek.

"Good morning, Val."

"I want to know all the details, but it can wait until we're seated." She grabbed my hand and pulled me toward the door.

Coffee and mimosas ordered, Val said, "Okay, now spill. I want every last detail."

I chuckled. "Wow, you're never gonna change, are you?"

"Hey, you love me just as I am. Why should I change at this point?"

"Ya got me there," I said, smiling. "It was nice. Very nice. We went to Fiddler's, but we didn't sit at the bar."

"Wow," Val interrupted. "I'm sure there was some whispering going on."

"Dennis kinda gave me the eye as we walked past the bar but didn't say anything. I picked Fiddler's because it's comfortable, and I could relax there, but sitting at the bar really wouldn't work for a date, and that's what this was, so we sat toward the back. Madison was our server."

I continued to relay the details of my date with Travis to Val, and when I got to the part where he kissed me, her eyes were like saucers.

"Wow!" she exclaimed. "Were you expecting that?"

"Not really, but I wasn't opposed to it either. It was … nice."

"Nice? That's it?"

"Don't get me wrong, I liked it, but frankly, it's the first time I've been kissed by someone other than Kar, so it felt a bit odd," I confessed. "On the other hand, I wouldn't mind doing it again. Maybe even more." I smiled.

"I'm happy for you, Beck." Val's voice was soft. "You deserve to be happy again." She sipped her mimosa and said, "So I'm thinking you'll see him again?"

"Yeah. He texted me this morning, and I'm going to his

house for dinner Thursday evening. And soon, I'd like the three of us to do something together. Maybe pizza and game night at my place some Saturday. After all, if I'm going to date him, I want the two of you to spend some time together too."

"I'd like that."

# twenty-three

TRAVIS

I woke the morning after my date with Beck feeling incredibly happy. I'd slept well, the memory of my time spent with that beautiful man in the forefront of my mind. My decision to kiss him good night had been impulsive, for sure, but I didn't regret it, and I hoped Beck didn't either.

As I prepared a breakfast of toast and coffee for myself, I thought of what I could make when I invited Beck over for dinner this week. I had been honest when I told him I wasn't much of a cook, but my grandmother did teach me a few things. Deciding on burgers and Grandma's killer potato salad, I quickly put together a shopping list, then texted Beck.

> I had a great time last night. And I meant it when I said I wanted you to come over this week. Would Thursday night work for you?

A few moments passed, and then I saw his reply.

> I enjoyed myself, too. Especially the kiss good night. Thursday is perfect. Can I bring anything?

I answered:

> Just your appetite. Nothing fancy—I hope you like burgers and potato salad. Let's say 7.

He closed with:

> I can't wait. C U then.

———

I SPENT Thursday morning cleaning my home. Just a living room, dining area, kitchen, two bedrooms, and two baths. Not large, but it was all mine, left to me by my grandmother. Don't get me wrong, I cleaned it regularly, but I didn't have folks over very often—well, except for Tony, but he was more like family at this point, so I didn't always clean for him—and tonight was special.

Once the house was tidied up to my satisfaction, I retreated to the kitchen to do some prep work. I'd already cooked the potatoes and hard boiled the eggs last night, just like Grandma always did, with a splash of oil and garlic powder in the potato water—don't ask me why, it's just how she did it, and that was good enough for me. I chopped onion and celery, along with some bell peppers, gave the eggs a coarse chop, then peeled the potatoes and cut them into chunks.

Finally, I mixed it all together with some mayonnaise and a splash or two of apple cider vinegar and some salt and pepper.

My grandmother never measured anything, so I didn't either. I'd learned to eyeball it long ago, tasting it along the way until it was right. I set the bowl in the fridge so the flavors could "get cozy" as my grandmother would say.

Then I turned to the burgers. I liked to season the meat with some salt and pepper, garlic powder, and some finely chopped onion. Plus a dash of Worcestershire sauce because that gave it a little zing. Once everything was mixed together, I formed the meat into two patties, set them on a plate, and stuck it in the fridge to mellow until I was ready to cook.

Satisfied that all the food was ready, I sat in my comfy chair in the corner of the living room. I was excited but a bit anxious about Beck coming over. I hadn't dated anyone in a very long time, and while I liked where we were going with this, frankly, I was a bit scared. Time for some meditation. I grounded and centered myself—once I had learned that from Auntie Mae, I figured out that meditation was so much easier for me—and concentrated on my breathing. I felt myself relax and rid my body of the stress that I had been building.

———

AT EXACTLY SEVEN, the doorbell rang. Beck stood there, looking as handsome as ever, holding a bouquet of wildflowers. "Hi. I know you said I didn't need to bring anything, but I couldn't come empty-handed," he said, handing me the blooms.

"They're gorgeous. Thank you," I replied. "Please, come in."

"You have a very beautiful home," he said, scanning the space.

"Thanks. It was my grandmother's; she left it to me. I've

done my best to keep it looking good. I wouldn't want her coming back to yell at me for letting the place fall apart." I smiled, hoping he'd catch on that I was joking. Grandma had moved on years ago.

We sat at the island in the kitchen, and I offered him a beverage.

"Whatever you're having," he said. I opened two non-alcoholic beers and placed one in front of him.

"I can tell you're not serious, but I have to ask," he said quietly. "Did your grandmother's spirit visit you after she passed?"

"Just once," I revealed. This wasn't something I usually talked about with anyone. "Shortly after she died, she came here one day to tell me that she loved me and to always follow my heart. Then she said she was moving on to the next plane."

"That must have been difficult for you, knowing that you'd never see her again."

"It was, but in some ways, I was happy for her, knowing that she'd truly be at peace," I said, sighing. "My only regret is that I never really got the chance to tell her how sorry I was that I didn't pay enough attention to what she was trying to tell me back then."

"You said something about that once before. Did something happen between the two of you?"

"No." I smiled sadly. "I was just a rebellious kid who thought I didn't have to listen to what she was trying to teach me."

"I think we all go through that at some point in our lives."

"Yeah, well, I agree that most kids do, but I think I gave her an extra-hard time." I didn't really want to share my story just yet, but hell, Beck had a right to know before things got too serious between us. "My folks died when I was a teenager. Dad had a stroke when I was just fifteen and never really recovered from it. Then he had another one about six months later, and ... he was gone." I took a swig of my beer before continuing.

"Look." Beck put his hand over mine. "You don't need to talk about this if it's too difficult. But I'm happy to listen."

"It's fine," I replied. "My mom never really got over Dad's death and just kind of pined away. She was gone less than a year later. We always said she died of a broken heart."

"That's awful. I'm so sorry, Travis."

"Thanks. Anyway, I'd been hearing voices and seeing spirits since I was about eight years old, but my folks didn't really want to hear about that stuff. I think my dad believed because his mom had a bit of the gift, but Mom said it frightened her, and she didn't want me saying anything about it. Especially to anyone at school. I think she was afraid they'd think I was crazy or something."

"I can see how that might be alarming to some folks," I offered.

"Yeah, well, Grandma would always listen, and that helped me, I dunno, accept it, I guess. But it got a little more intense and frequent after my folks passed. I don't think it was because of that, I just think that as I grew up, I was more attuned to those on the other plane. But I had also begun acting out a bit, in part because I was having a hard time dealing with my parents' deaths, but also because I really didn't have many friends. Of course, I was also just at that age where I thought I knew better than any adults, especially my grandma."

"I can't imagine how you were feeling back then. It had to have been traumatic," Beck said gently.

"Looking back on it all, I was a real bastard to my grandmother."

"I'm sure she forgave you for anything you think you did."

"You're probably right, but I still feel bad. I was an idiot, and in many ways, I paid for how I treated her."

"How?"

"The drinking. See, because I didn't really pay attention to what she tried to tell me, I didn't understand some of the basics about using my gift. So when I came in contact with spirits and tried to help them move on, I tended to leak energy. Sometimes a lot. And then I'd get exhausted and need lots of time to recuperate. Also, some days the voices are louder than others. I'm not sure why, but it can be hard to ignore them. I started drinking since that quieted the voices."

"But you've learned how to prevent all of that?"

"Yeah. I met with Auntie Mae. She's got some of the gift as well and taught me things like grounding and centering myself. That helps quiet the voices to some degree, and it also helps me contain my energy better." I sighed, shaking my head. "If I'd listened to Grandma all those years ago, I could have been better at this."

"Hey," Beck said, reaching over to touch my hand. "I appreciate you sharing all that, and I really think your grandma would be happy knowing that you finally did something about it. Now, moving the conversation to lighter topics, I think you promised me a burger and some amazing potato salad." He winked, and I could only chuckle.

"You're absolutely right. Time to eat!"

# twenty-four

BECK

"Oh my God, that was fabulous." I groaned at the thought of how much I'd eaten. "And I agree, your grandmother's potato salad is the best I've ever had."

"Thank you." Travis smiled warmly. "It's really simple to make, but oh so comforting."

I helped him clean up the kitchen, and we retired to the living room. We both sat on the sofa, close but not exactly touching, and Travis asked, "Wanna watch some TV or just chat?"

Rather than answer directly, I said, "Thanks for dinner. It was delicious." I stared at him for a moment, wondering if I should do what I'd been thinking about since I'd arrived at his home. The gleam in his eyes seemed to speak volumes. I could tell he wanted this as much as I did. I leaned over and kissed him gently on the lips. One kiss turned into two, then three. I loved the feeling of his soft lips on mine, his chest pressed against my own. When I felt the tip of his tongue glide along the seam of my lips, I readily opened up to him, greedily sucking on his tongue.

Travis straddled my lap, and I felt his hardness press against my own. I ran my fingers through his dark locks, deepening our kisses even more. I couldn't get close enough to this man. This was happening fast, but God, it felt so good, so right. *But too fast?* After a few minutes, we came up for air.

"Wow," Travis exclaimed, panting.

"Yeah." I grinned.

He leaned forward, pressing our foreheads together. "If you haven't gotten the message yet, I like you, Beck. A lot."

"I like you too, Travis," I began.

"Uh-oh." His voice fell. "I sense a 'but' coming."

"It's not that I don't want this, that I don't want you," I said. "But I would like to slow down just a little. I'm sorry." I hoped he could hear the care in my words. I really did want more to happen between us, but part of me was still scared.

"I'm the one who's sorry," Travis said quietly. "I shouldn't have pushed myself on you."

"You didn't," I reassured him. "I'm feeling it too, but you need to understand, you're the first person I've been with since Kar died. And even though he said that he thinks the two of us would be good together, this is kind of a big deal for me. I mean, um, ah, shit, I'm not explaining this correctly at all."

"No. It's okay, I get it. You need more time."

"Just a little. But I want to keep on seeing you. And kissing you if that's okay." I felt the heat rise in my face. "I'm just not sure when I'll be ready for more."

Travis got a strange look on his face and turned to stare off toward his kitchen.

"What is it?" I asked.

"Kar," he replied. "He's here." Travis pointed. I followed his gaze, and for a brief moment, saw a flicker of Kar's face.

"Kar!" I cried. "What are you doing here?"

"He says that he's tried to keep his distance, only checking in once in a while to make sure you are okay," Travis told me. "But he thinks his presence is distracting to you. He says you seem afraid that he's gonna pop in like this, and that freaks you out."

"Yeah," I confessed, chagrined. "It does. You still know me so well, Kar," I said to the empty space before me, hoping that Kar was still standing there.

"Kar says he's doesn't want to make either one of us uncomfortable, so he's decided to leave."

"What, no! Kar, please don't leave yet; I'm not ready!" I couldn't hide the anguish in my voice.

"Not permanently," Travis said, now speaking for Kar. "I'm not moving to the next plane yet. The anniversary of my death is next week, and while I thought I might take that opportunity to move on, I've decided that I'm not quite ready either. I'm just going to make myself scarce so that the two of you can enjoy some time together. But Samhain is little more than a month away. The veil between planes is especially thin then, which will make it a little easier to move to the next plane. If all goes well, I'll move on at that time. But I promise, I'll come to see you both before that happens."

"If you think that's best," I said weakly. Even though I was scared and confused when Kar first showed up, I had to admit, I'd gotten kind of used to knowing he was around.

"It is, my love," Travis said, still relaying Kar's words. "You and Travis need time together without you worrying that I'll show up unexpectedly. I see the possibility between the two of you. I need you to see it too. And now I'll take my leave." Travis slumped against the sofa's back cushion.

"Are you okay, Travis?" I reached for his hand.

"Yeah," he answered. "It just happened so quickly, I barely had time to center myself. It almost felt like Kar had taken over my vocal cords or something. Took a bit out of me."

"He's really gone now, right?"

"He is. I don't feel him anywhere nearby."

We sat together holding hands for a while. Neither of us quite knew what to say.

"I meant what I said before," I said. "Despite the um, little interruption from my deceased husband, I do want to see you again."

Then after a chaste kiss good night, I made my way home.

---

WHEN I GOT HOME, I was still feeling a bit rattled by Kar's appearance, so I poured myself a shot of bourbon and sat in my recliner, thinking about everything that had happened that night.

Yes, the food was amazing. But that wasn't what was filling my thoughts.

The kissing was really nice even if it got a bit heated rather quickly. I had been completely honest with Travis when I told him I wanted more, but that I needed to slow down. As right as everything felt, the memory of Kar was holding me back a little. The romantic part of me felt like I was being unfaithful to Kar even though my logical brain said that was bullshit. I'd need to figure out how to move past that if I expected to have a future with Travis. *Whoa!* A future with Travis? Yeah, if I was being completely honest with myself, that was where this was headed.

Kar showing up had been quite freaky at first. But I guess I understood why he'd be keeping an eye on me. After all, he'd admitted he had been doing that for a while. And he did say that he thought Travis and I had a future together. I guess that meant we had Kar's blessing to pursue whatever was happening between us. Now I just had to get my romantic brain on board with that idea.

I finished the bourbon in my glass and rinsed it out in the kitchen. "Well," I said aloud to no one at all, "I'll just have to sleep on it, I guess."

---

"How was your date last night?" Val asked when she walked into the pharmacy the next morning.

"Fine," I replied, knowing she'd want all the details. "But can you curtail your curiosity until we meet at Fiddler's tonight after work? I really don't want to get into the details here."

"Okay."

Fortunately, work was steady all day, and before we knew it, we were heading out the door.

"See you there," Val called out, climbing into her MINI Cooper.

As Dennis made our drinks, Val turned to me. "Okay, spill."

I relayed the events of the previous evening, sipping my bourbon occasionally. It was amusing to watch Val's eyes widen as the story went on.

"Wow," she whispered when I finished. "So what happens now?"

"We're definitely gonna see each other again although we

haven't made any specific plans yet," I told her. "I'll call or text Travis and ask him out next week."

"Do you really think Kar is going to stay away for a while?"

"I do. He basically said that he thinks Travis and I belong together, and he wants to give us time without him around. And I know Travis believes him too."

"Do you think that will help with your whole 'cheating on Kar' bullshit?" Val air quoted.

"What do you mean, bullshit?"

"Look, Beck," she began. "I know you loved Kar. Still love him, in fact. And there's nothing wrong with that. But hell, it's been five years. Don't you think you can love someone else while still keeping Kar in your heart? Caring for Travis doesn't negate your feelings for Kar. I know you have enough room in your heart for both."

It was as if a lightbulb had just gone off above my head. "You're absolutely right. I've been thinking about this over and over again, but you were able to put into words what I couldn't. Yes, I can love both of them, can't I?"

# twenty-five

TRAVIS

MY PHONE RANG Monday morning just as I was finishing the breakfast dishes. I'd been thinking about my conversation with Beck the day before—and our plans for dinner on Tuesday—and almost missed the call. It wasn't a number I recognized, so I answered professionally, "Travis Watson, Paranormal Investigations."

"Hello," a frantic male voice replied. "There's some weird shit happening in my bookstore. A friend suggested I call you. Can you help me?"

"What kind of weird stuff is going on?" I asked.

"Oh, books flying off shelves, chairs in the sitting area moving around at night when no one's there. And the other day, the faucet in the restroom just turned on all by itself," the man said. "My friend said it sounds like a poltergeist, and that you could get rid of it for me."

"I'm happy to come to your shop and see what I can do." I quoted my rates and asked for the address.

I arrived at the bookstore about twenty minutes later and met Geoff, the owner. "I've kept the shop closed, at least for this morning, but I can't do that for too long."

"I get it." I grounded and centered myself, then stretched out my senses. "I can tell you right now," I said, "there's definitely a presence here. If you can stay by the door and let me roam around a bit, I should know more in a little while."

I slowly walked down the first section of books, trying to get a sense of where this spirit was. When I got to the next aisle, one of the books on an upper shelf flew past me, narrowly missing my head. I turned, looking with my inner eye for the culprit.

"I know you're here," I said quietly. "What do you want?" More books flew off shelves, and then, very faintly, I heard a voice in my head: *Leave me alone.*

As I had feared, this was gonna take a while.

———

It had taken so much longer than I anticipated. After much discussion and cajoling, I finally managed to get the entity, a woman who called herself Amelia, to leave the bookstore. I still wasn't exactly clear on why she picked that place to haunt—a lot of what she said was mangled and disjointed—but I surmised that something bad had happened to her there a long time ago. She recently returned to get vengeance, not really understanding that what happened involved different people than the ones she was tormenting.

Rather than just go on her merry way, or move to the next plane, Amelia decided to hang out with me. Great. Just what I needed. This had only happened to me once before, and when I failed to engage the spirit, they got bored and left after an hour or so. Amelia, however, wouldn't take silence for an answer. She chattered on endlessly about nonsense that I knew nothing about. And no matter what I did, I couldn't quiet her voice in my head. None of the techniques I'd learned from Auntie Mae helped.

So I took the coward's way out. I stopped at the corner liquor store and bought a bottle of my buddy Jack. As in Daniels. I knew it was wrong, but I was out of sorts, my head was pounding, and I couldn't think straight.

The first swig quieted Amelia's voice a bit. Another sip, even more. By the time I'd emptied a third of the bottle, I could barely hear her. I passed out on the sofa.

———

SUN STREAMING in the front windows woke me the following morning. My head was pounding, and Amelia was still yapping. Without thinking, I stole a sip of Jack straight from the bottle that sat on the floor beside the sofa. This led to another sip and then a third. Yeah, this was why I shouldn't use alcohol to quiet the damned voices—I just don't know when to stop. As a result, I was in and out of consciousness much of the day. But at least I couldn't hear Amelia!

I heard bells. Why was I hearing bells? I woke still groggy, trying to remember where I was. Oh, yeah, the couch in my living room. I'd somehow managed to drool on the T-shirt I was wearing but couldn't muster up the feelings to really care about that. What was that incessant ringing? Oh, wait, it was the doorbell.

I staggered to the front door and pulled it open to find

Beck standing there, looking all handsome and hot. *Fuck!* It all came back to me in a rush. We had a date planned for tonight.

"Travis? Are you all right?" The concern in his voice hit me like a deluge of icy water.

"Shit," I said weakly. "I seriously fucked up, Beck. I'm sorry."

"Whaddya mean you fucked up? What's wrong?"

"Come in and I'll explain."

Beck walked to the sofa and picked up the bottle of Jack Daniels. It was almost empty. "I'm guessing this has something to do with your current condition?" He kept his tone steady; I couldn't tell exactly how pissed he was at that point.

"Yeah," I said, rubbing the back of my neck. I looked at my stockinged feet, unwilling to meet his eyes. He sat on the club chair; I took the end of the sofa.

"So, tell me what happened." His voice was calm and oh so quiet.

"I had the worst day ever yesterday," I began. I recounted the events at the bookstore, leaving nothing out. "Then because I couldn't bear to listen to Amelia's never-ending babbling, I made a bad decision and picked up that bottle on my way home." I shook my head, wishing a hole would open up and swallow me so I could avoid the embarrassing predicament I had found myself in.

"I see."

It grew uncomfortably quiet.

"I wouldn't blame you if you want to walk out that door and never see me again," I choked out, dreading Beck's reply.

"Hey, look at me," he said gently. I slowly lifted my chin and met his gaze. I only saw concern. "I'm not angry. But I was scared because I didn't know if something had happened to you. We haven't known each other for very long, but I thought there was something happening between us. Why didn't you call me? Or Tony for that matter? You said that he's a close friend. Why didn't you ask for help?"

"I was afraid," I said honestly. "And ashamed. This is my job, and I should be able to handle it, but deep down, I'm just a coward, I guess. You've probably figured it out already, but I don't let people in very much. I've been kinda screwed up all my life and don't like folks to know just how much." I knew I sounded whiny, but at that point, I really didn't care. "And besides, you were still at work. It wouldn't be right for me to call you there."

"Well, if we're gonna keep seeing each other, this bullshit needs to stop. I'm here for you. I want to make sure you know that. And I don't care that I was working. If you need me, I'll do my best to help you however I can."

Beck moved to sit beside me and wrapped his arms around me. I turned, pressing my face into his shoulder, and sobbed. He just held me, whispering, "That's it. Let it all out."

After several minutes, I collected myself and pulled away, looking Beck straight in the eye. "Thank you," I said sincerely. "Ever since Grandma died, I really haven't had anyone I could lean on."

"Well, now you've got me," Beck replied. "Now, how about you get yourself cleaned up, and then maybe we can salvage the rest of our date night? But first, is Amelia still here?"

"I can't hear her. Or feel her presence. Maybe I ignored her enough that she finally gave up and left. And seriously, I don't deserve you. Oh, I may have slobbered all over your shirt." I pointed to his shoulder.

"Good. We don't need anyone else here right now. We

don't have to go out. We can order something in. And the shirt will be good as new once it's laundered. Now scoot."

I grabbed some take-out menus from a drawer in the kitchen and handed them to Beck. "Take your pick. All these places deliver." I headed to the bathroom to shower. *How did I get so lucky as to find a man like Beck?*

# twenty-six

BECK

I WAS WRUNG OUT. I got home from my date with Travis filled with so many emotions. Based on what I'd just witnessed, involving Travis's misuse of alcohol, I shouldn't have poured myself a drink, but that's exactly what I did. *Dammit!* After what had happened that evening, I thought I deserved it.

I sat, sipped, and went over everything in my head. We'd talked over the weekend and agreed to go out for a quick bite to eat Tuesday evening. I'd tried calling him when I left work, but there was no answer. I just figured he was in the shower or something. But then it took almost five minutes of my ringing his doorbell, and I started to worry.

I was so relieved when he finally answered the door that I don't think I had time to be angry. I wasn't happy that he'd been drinking to excess, but he realized that he'd fucked up, and I saw that as a good thing. He might not know it yet, but we were gonna talk more about this subject at some point. I was determined to help in any way I could.

———

WE WERE SLAMMED all day at work on Wednesday, so Val and I didn't have a free moment to chat. As we walked out of work together, she said, "Come sit in my car for a minute, Beck." Naturally, I did as I was told.

"What's up, Val?" I tried to play innocent.

"Don't give me that shit, Beck. We didn't have a chance to talk at all today, but I can tell something's up. What's wrong? Something with Travis?"

I told her everything that had happened the night before. I'll give her credit: her facial expressions showed alarm and concern, but she didn't interrupt me.

"I want to help him with this," I admitted.

"So you still care for him?"

"I do. Frankly, my feelings have only gotten stronger. This changes nothing."

"Okay, then I'm in too. Whatever you or Travis need, I'm here for you." See, this is why Val and I are BFFs.

"Thanks, Val," I said honestly. "I want to invite Travis to one of our Saturday game nights at my house. Would you be okay if I asked him to join us this week? I want you to get to know him better, and I think a fun evening together will help."

"That's fine with me. What were you thinking of playing?"

"My first thought was Five Crowns. If Travis isn't familiar with it, it's easy enough to learn. I'll order pizza for dinner. Just an easy, relaxing evening together."

———

THE DOORBELL RANG JUST as I was coming down the stairs.

"Hey," Travis said when I opened the door. "I'm not too early, am I?"

"Not at all. Val should be here any minute." As Travis entered, he turned toward me and leaned forward. I automatically met him halfway. The kiss was sweet.

"Sorry," Travis said, "but I've wanted to do that since we last saw each other on Tuesday."

"Never apologize for kissing me," I told him. "I happen to like kissing."

"Noted." He smiled and followed me into the kitchen.

"Would you like something to drink?"

"Just some club soda with lime if you have it." He sounded embarrassed.

"Hey, no judgment. Remember, I'm here for you."

"Um, does Val know?"

"Yeah. I hope that's okay. I pretty much tell her everything that happens in my life. It's the kind of relationship we have."

"That's fine. And please, don't *not* drink on my behalf."

Just then, Val walked in the back door. "Hi, boys," she said, hugging me and bussing my cheek. She turned to Travis and asked, "Are hugs okay with you?" He nodded, and she continued, "Good, 'cause I'm a hugger," and proceeded to wrap him in her arms.

"It's good to see you again, Val," Travis told her.

"Same. And I'll tell you the same thing I told Beck on Wednesday. I'm here for you both. Whatever you need."

"Thanks, Val. That means a lot."

"Well, Beck likes you, and I'm assuming you like Beck, so that makes you family." Travis was speechless; his eyes glistened, and I could tell that he was moved by Val's words.

"What are you drinking?" I asked Val, trying to stop us from getting too serious.

"Nothing yet," she sassed.

"Don't abstain on my account," Travis added.

"Well, then, some red wine would be lovely, sweetie. Can we eat first, please? I'm famished."

"Sure. Usually, we play for a while, then eat," I explained to Travis. "But apparently we're changing that up tonight." I looked pointedly at Val. I was just trying to rile her up since I really didn't care when we ate. But it was fun to push Val's buttons. "Do you want some cheese and crackers while we wait?" I asked Val. "You know where everything is." I gestured around the room. "Travis, what kind of pizza do you like?"

"Anything except anchovies. And I love extra cheese."

"Oh, you're gonna fit in here just fine," Val told him, grinning. She squeezed his shoulder as she headed for the fridge to look for cheese.

"The pizza should be here in about a half hour," I announced, putting my tablet away. "So, Travis, have you ever played Five Crowns?"

"No, I haven't."

"No problem. I'll explain the rules while we wait for the pizza, and then we can play a few practice hands so you get the idea." As I spoke, I took the special deck of cards, along with a pad of score sheets, out of a kitchen drawer. "Let's start with the basics. Do you know how to play rummy?"

"I do, but it's been a while."

"So, Five Crowns is based on rummy, where you make sets of the same card or runs of the same suit. But it uses a special deck that has a fifth suit called stars." I continued my explanation and then dealt a few hands to show him how it all worked.

"Okay," Travis said after the third practice hand. "I'm getting the hang of it now."

When the doorbell rang, Val said, "I'll get it."

"I paid online when I ordered," I told her as she headed down the hall, "including the tip." I grabbed plates and napkins and placed everything on the island. Val returned with the pies, and we dug in.

After demolishing two large pizzas, we settled in for a fun evening of cards and conversation. Even though this was Travis's first time playing Five Crowns, he fared quite well, beating me by a few points. But Val reigned supreme as she often did.

———

"Oh my God, I didn't realize how late it was!" Val exclaimed when we finished the second game.

"It's only ten thirty," I replied. Val looked at me knowingly, her eyes wide, an almost evil smile on her face.

"I'm meeting my friend Erin for brunch in the morning, so I really should be going." She stood, snatching her coat off the hook by the back door. "It was great hanging out with you, Travis. We need to do this again."

"I enjoyed it, and sure, I'd love to get together with you both another time."

"Beck and I meet up for brunch regularly too. We try to do it at least once a month. Make sure he invites you next time."

"I'm standing right here," I deadpanned.

"Well, then you know what to do." Val smiled.

She gave hugs and kisses and was out the door in a flash.

"Is it me, or was she trying to give us some alone time?"

Travis stepped closer and kissed me. "Thank God she

finally left." He grinned. "I've been waiting to do that all night."

"You could kiss me in front of Val. I mean, she *has* seen two men kiss before."

"True, but I was afraid that if I kissed you, it might lead to other things?"

"Well, then." I took his hand and led him into the den. "Let's see what we can do about that."

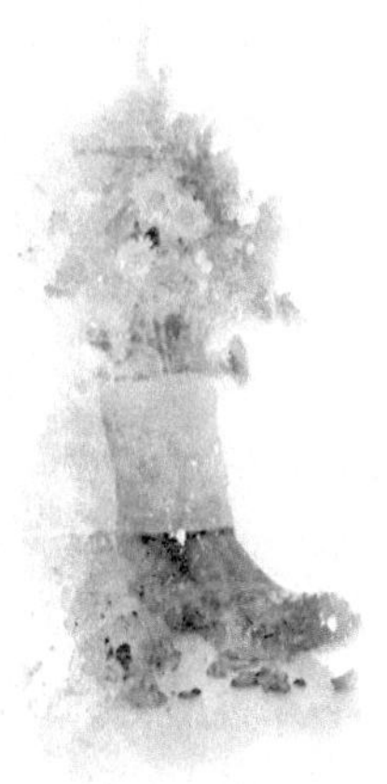

# twenty-seven

BECK

I sat on the sofa, and Travis straddled me, kissing me deeply. *God, I want him!* I groaned into his mouth, hoping to relay how much I was enjoying this. I ground my pelvis against him, feeling him lengthen along my own hard dick.

"Want you so much," Travis panted when we finally came up for air.

I swung my legs around, taking Travis with me. He was now spread on top of me, our bodies touching in all the right places. "Want you too," I moaned, kissing Travis again.

Travis reached for the top button of my shirt, and when I didn't stop him, he unfastened it and moved to the next one. Soon, my shirt was open as Travis ogled my hairy chest.

"Mmmm." He drew his finger through the dark curls and scooted down a bit, sucking one of my nipples into his mouth. He pulled the shirttails from my jeans, giving him better access to my torso. As his fingers trailed to my belt buckle, he whispered, "Is this okay?"

"Yes, please," I begged.

Travis slowly undid my belt, then unbuttoned my jeans. As he slid the zipper down, he ran his finger along my fabric-encased cock. A moan escaped my lips. I lifted my ass, and Travis slid my jeans down to my knees and put his mouth on my still-covered dick. He huffed, resulting in an even louder moan from me. Carefully lifting the waistband of my navy boxer briefs, Travis revealed my thick cock, which was surrounded by a nicely trimmed patch of dark curls.

Travis tucked the waistband under my balls, then licked up the length of my rigid dick, teasing my frenulum when he reached the head.

"If you keep that up, I'm gonna come," I panted.

"Um, that's the point, isn't it?" Travis asked.

"Smartass. I just don't want it to be over too soon."

"Not to worry." Travis stood and quickly shed his shirt and pants, then bent and pulled my jeans completely off. He knelt between my legs and leaned over to kiss me yet again.

I wrapped my arms around him in a hug, then slid my hands down his back and under the waistband of his briefs, cupping his ass and pulling him closer.

Travis broke the kiss and whispered, "I wanna suck your cock."

I chuckled. "Only if I get a turn too."

"I think we can make that happen."

"Before we continue," I began, "want to move this to somewhere a bit more comfortable?" Needing no further encouragement, we grabbed our clothes, and I pulled him upstairs to my bedroom.

We fell on the bed, our garments scattered. I turned so that we were mouth to cock, lying side by side. As Travis licked the head of my cock, I ran my tongue around the crown of his. I sucked and teased, licked him, and fondled his balls. I moaned around him as he sucked, relishing the feel of his hot mouth on me.

I paused a moment to wet my middle finger, then went back to my ministrations. I reached behind his furry balls and located his pucker, tapping and playing along the rim. I pushed gently against his hole as I sped up on his cock. After a few moments, I felt his balls tighten and knew he was close.

"Gonna come!" he shouted before taking my cock to the back of his throat.

Feeling my own climax approaching, I sucked and licked even more until I felt his release on my tongue. I barely had time to swallow it all before I came, then glanced down to see him lapping at my cock greedily. I licked at some cum that I'd missed earlier and kissed the head of his cock.

As our breathing slowed, I murmured, "Mmmm, that was wonderful."

"Yeah, it was," Travis agreed.

We dozed off for a little while, and when we woke up, Travis said he was going to go home. We showered together, and after Travis left, I fell back into bed. I'd half thought about asking him to stay over, but I needed a little bit of space after what had happened. Not that I regretted anything Travis and I had done. On the contrary, I felt really good about it. No regrets, no shame. I hadn't thought about Kar once, and I didn't feel guilty about that either. Huh. Part of me wanted to let that sink in.

There in bed, waiting for sleep to once again overtake me, I came to the conclusion that I was finally ready to move on. In fact, it seemed I already had.

———

I HAD JUST FINISHED lunch when my phone rang. I recognized the ringtone as Val's.

"Hey, sweetie, how was brunch with Erin?" I greeted her. Val and Erin had been childhood friends who'd lost touch with one another at one point. They'd connected again several years ago and had reforged their friendship.

"Lovely. We really haven't spent any time together for a while, so we got caught up. She says hello, by the way."

"I'm glad you had a good time."

"And what about you? Did you and Travis have a good time after I left last night?"

"We did, actually. Thanks for asking."

"Ooh, tell me more!" Val's voice rose in excitement.

"Now, Val, you know I don't kiss and tell!" I feigned shock.

"Fine. Without giving me all the juicy details, tell me what you can."

So I did. Well, almost. After all, Val was like my sister, so *without* going into all the intimate details, I told her enough so that she'd understand things were moving forward between Travis and me.

———

I SPENT the rest of the day at my desk, working on my latest story. Surprisingly, the writing came easily. Since I'd experienced my own intimacy with Travis, the characters in my story now had lots to say and do.

As I sat reading in bed that evening, my thoughts once again turned to the time I'd spent with Travis the night before. I hadn't heard from him today. I supposed he was giving me some space. Also, it seemed that my dead husband knew what he was doing when he suggested that Travis and I belonged together.

# twenty-eight

TRAVIS

My phone buzzed as I drove into town. I hadn't seen Tony for a while, so I was heading to the Raven's Claw for a visit. Once I'd parked in the lot behind the row of shops, I saw the text from Beck.

> Good morning. Hope you have a fantastic day.

I wasn't sure when it started, or who started it exactly, but in the past couple of weeks, we'd begun to text each other at random times during the day. It was our way of touching base with each other, and I got a tingly feeling in my stomach every time I got a message from him.

> I hope your day is amazing too. Talk later.

Sending my reply, I sauntered to the nearby café, my steps suddenly lighter.

"Oh my God, you *are* still alive!" Tony exclaimed as I entered the shop carrying two beverages.

"You're a funny man, Tone," I said, handing him a take-out cup of tea. "It hasn't been *that* long."

"Has there been a spike in paranormal activity that I haven't noticed, or are things going that well with the new man in your life?"

It was true I hadn't been to the store in a while, but I *had* spoken to Tony not that long ago and told him of the recent developments between Beck and me.

"Things are really good between us," I explained. "In fact, I'd like the two of you to meet. After all, you're the two most important people in my life."

"That means a lot," Tony said quietly, emotion coloring his words. "And I'd love to meet Beck. How about Saturday? You could come by the shop."

"I'll check with Beck, but yeah, that could work. I'll let you know." I sipped at my coffee. "And to answer your other question, no, there hasn't been an increase in paranormal activity, but business has been good lately. Not sure what it is about Massachusetts, but we do seem to attract our share of the weird."

"I blame all those witches in Salem ages ago. I think they cursed the state or something. But hey, it's my livelihood too, so I'm not complaining."

———

WHEN I HAD VISITED Tony the previous day, he'd given me the name of a gentleman who'd called him about a disturbance in his home. I'd spoken to the man this morning and had agreed to check it out. It turned out to be the ghost of the previous owner. He'd passed shortly after his wife and had been roaming around, looking for her and causing a bit of mischief along the way. I searched the area but couldn't locate any spirit that might be his wife, and he finally agreed to move to the next plane.

I thought about that spirit—his name was Frank—as I drove home. He was so lost without his spouse, just searching everywhere he could think of. I found it quite sad, and it reminded me how lucky I was to finally have someone in my life that I cared about and who cared about me. I hoped that I had helped Frank when I explained that it was likely his wife had already crossed over and that he'd find her on the other side.

At home, I fixed myself some dinner. I was tired but not as tired as I would have been before I met Auntie Mae. Using the techniques that she had shown me kept most of my spiritual energy safely in my body so that the fatigue was manageable. I was just settling in on the couch after my meal when my phone rang.

"Hey, Beck. How was work today?" This was another recent development between us. One of us would invariably call the other almost every evening.

"It was good," Beck replied. "Not too crazy but steady enough that the day passed quickly. How was your day?"

I told him about Frank and the search for his wife, Lillian.

"That's so sad, not being able to find a loved one."

"I felt exactly the same way. I just hope I helped him."

"I'm sure you did. You're a good man, Travis."

I didn't accept compliments well, so I changed the subject. "I saw Tony yesterday morning and was telling him that I'd like the two of you to meet. I also wanted to get you a crystal or two while we're there. Well, if that's something you'd be interested in." I played with the amulets hanging around my neck. "How about we swing by his shop on Saturday?"

"I'd like that. What time were you thinking?" Beck queried. "I can pick you up, and we can drive over together."

"Hmmm, actually, I was wondering if you wanted to come over for dinner Friday night? If you stayed over, we could just head over whenever we wanted."

"A sleepover, huh?" Humor coated his words. "That sounds like a wonderful idea."

We chatted for a few more minutes, then said our good-byes. *Oh my God, Beck was gonna stay over!* I hoped no one had a paranormal emergency on Friday—I needed to clean the bedroom and change the sheets.

———

THE BEDROOM WAS SPOTLESS. Vacuumed and dusted to within an inch of its life along with a clean set of bed linens, it looked better than it had in ages. I didn't normally have guests who stayed over, so I didn't always give the room the attention it deserved. But now all my clothes were hung up or in the clothes hamper, and it felt good to have a tidy room. I might get used to this.

I tossed the dirty sheets into the washing machine and decided to tackle the bathroom next. I kept it reasonably neat, but since I was having a special visitor, I thought a full cleaning was in order. A glance at the clock in the kitchen as I exited the laundry room assured me that I had plenty of time to finish the bathroom before showering. Beck had said he'd go home to shower and change after work, so he likely wouldn't be here before seven o'clock or so. We'd agreed on Chinese takeout from the place nearby, so I didn't have the added stress of cooking tonight.

I had just slipped into my jeans and a black, long-sleeved T-shirt when the doorbell rang.

"Hi," I said, leaning in for a kiss when I opened the door. "Come in."

Before shedding his coat, he kissed me again and smiled. "I've missed you."

"Me too," I agreed. I hung up his jacket and asked, "How were things at work today?"

"Pretty good. Val says hi."

"I take it she knows you're staying over tonight?"

"Yeah." Beck chuckled. "She's thrilled about it, actually."

"And how about you?" I thought we should get our feelings out in the open.

"I'm excited, but honestly, I'm a little nervous too."

"Same," I said.

"Whew." Beck sighed. "I'm glad it's not just me. I mean, we've had our intimate moments, but we haven't done an overnight yet. It's a big step."

"Beck." I looked into his eyes. "It's fine if you're not ready. I don't want to pressure you into doing—"

He put a finger to my lips. "It's not that at all. I said yes when you asked because I *am* ready. I *want* to be with you." He replaced his finger with his lips, kissing me gently. "You're not pressuring me into anything."

Just then his stomach growled, breaking the serious mood. We both giggled like schoolkids, and I said, "Maybe now's a good time to order dinner."

# twenty-nine

BECK

As I SHOWERED in preparation for my evening out, I realized I was nervous. Sure, Travis and I had made out and given each other blow jobs and hand jobs over the past couple of weeks, but we hadn't gone any further than that. I hadn't had anal intercourse with anyone for five years—either giving or receiving. Not since Kar died. Well, I did have a toy, but it wasn't quite the same. And now here I was getting ready to visit Travis for dinner. And stay over. Yes, this was the night we'd do more than kiss and fondle each other.

After all, Kar actually gave his blessing to this. When I "spoke" to Kar the night he came to see us at Travis's house—God, it was weird to think that I actually talked to him through Travis—he told me he wanted this for me, and now that he knew I was moving on with my life, he was ready to move on too.

I could admit that I loved being with Travis; in many ways it felt like home. And I enjoyed the stuff we'd done so far. Travis was a warm and tender lover, and I was completely comfortable with him.

And now? I felt ready. I missed having someone in my life like this. I missed having someone to hug, to cuddle with. Since meeting Travis and accepting the fact that Kar was really here, encouraging me to find someone, I had realized how lonely I'd been for the past five years.

I toweled off, determined to allow the evening to unfold however it might. No pressure.

———

I PUT away the leftover food as Travis washed the few dishes we'd used. He wiped his hands on the dish towel, and I wrapped my arms around him, kissing him deeply.

"Mmm, Kung Pao chicken," I murmured against his lips, continuing to kiss him.

"Let's take this to the living room," he panted, "unless you'd like to lie down?"

I nodded, and he took my hand, leading me to his bedroom.

We continued making out on the bed, tongues probing and testing for dominance. My hand searched for the hem of his shirt, moving under and up, scraping my fingernails along his ribs. I reached a nipple and tweaked it gently until it pebbled at my touch.

Travis pulled off his shirt, and I licked at the chocolate nub, nibbling at it. He pulled me back up for a searing kiss, and as I pressed on top of him, I felt his arousal, hard against my thigh.

"Just so you know," he whispered, "there's no one else here. It's just you and me."

That thought hadn't entered my head, but somehow knowing we were truly alone comforted me. I found his belt buckle, unfastened it, and reached into his pants. Taking hold of his erection, I squeezed it lightly and felt it grow even harder.

Travis moaned into my mouth as we slowly undressed each other without breaking lip contact. Soon we were both naked, and I lined up our cocks, giving them a few tugs.

"Remember, no pressure," Travis told me. "I just want to be close to you."

"I want this," I said, wrapping my arms around him. "It's just been so long."

"It's okay, Beck. You set the pace."

I kissed him deeply, loving the friction of hair along our torsos. His cock was hard against my own, and as strange as it was to be with someone other than Kar, it felt so right. I pushed him onto his back and kissed my way down his chest, sucking on one nipple and then the other until they once again pebbled under my touch. But I wanted more.

I nibbled down his chest until I reached his gorgeous cock, the head already glistening with pre-cum. I lick it clean, dipping my tongue into his slit, then taking him to the back of my throat.

"Mmmm," he moaned as I hummed around his dick and sucked. Travis ran his fingers through my hair. After working on his cock for a few moments, I moved down, licking his balls. I lifted Travis's legs, pushing his knees to his chest while I kissed and nibbled my way to his hole. I laved his pucker, pushing in with my tongue, his moans urging me on. I loved eating his ass, and from the sounds coming from Travis, I knew he was enjoying it too.

"I want to feel you inside me," Travis panted.

I felt him move slightly, then hand me a condom and a bottle of lube. Pouring some lube on my fingers, I pushed one, then another into his eager hole.

"Ready now!" he cried.

"Don't wanna hurt you, babe." The endearment slipped out. *Huh, need to think about that later.*

His hand roamed the bed, searching for the condom, and finding it, he ripped it open, pulling me up quickly. He grabbed my rigid cock and unrolled the condom down its length. I slicked myself up with lube, pointing the head of my dick to his waiting hole. I eased in slowly, moving past the ring of muscle. His heat enveloped me.

Pulling my face toward him, Travis kissed me passionately as I began to thrust, pulling almost out, then plunging back in.

"You fill me up so good," Travis moaned. "So fucking good."

"I love how you feel wrapped around my cock," I said. "So hot and tight. Not gonna last."

"Come in me," Travis pleaded. "I want to feel it."

I felt Travis's hand move across my ass, and a finger slid into my crack. When the pad of his finger grazed my hole, I knew I was a goner. My orgasm hit me, and I filled the condom. My thrusts slowed, but I stayed inside him, relishing the closeness for just a moment longer.

I finally pulled out, holding the condom at the base of my dick. There were tissues on the nightstand, so I wrapped the used condom in one. That's when I noticed that my belly was covered with cum.

"I, um, I came right after you," Travis said quietly. "I hadn't even touched my dick. That's never happened to me before."

I couldn't think of an adequate response, so I grabbed a few more tissues to clean us up as best I could, kissed him, wrapped my arms around him, and fell into a peaceful slumber.

# thirty

TRAVIS

I woke suddenly, my arms wrapped around another body, playing the big spoon. It took me a moment to realize that it was Beck. He'd spent the night after we'd made love. There, I said it. *Well, thought it, actually.* It was more than just sex, at least it felt that way for me. He stirred in my arms, and I held him tighter, running my hand along his hairy belly.

"Hey," he groaned sleepily. "What time is it?"

"No idea. I just woke up myself. I don't wanna move, so I'm not checking right now." I nibbled at his ear. "How are you feeling this morning?"

"I'm good." He turned to face me, our chests—and more —rubbing together. "How are you?"

"I feel great. Last night was wonderful; I slept quite soundly with you in my arms."

"So, no regrets about what we did?" There was a hint of worry in his voice.

"None at all. You?"

"Surprisingly, no," he admitted, chuckling humorlessly. "It's strange. After Kar died, I always thought that if the day ever came that I met someone who I wanted this kind of intimacy with, I would feel something like sadness or regret. That it would somehow be unfaithful to Kar. That's why it was so difficult for me to actually try and date anyone. But this feels good. It feels right. It's funny, I'm aspiring to be a writer, but I can't come up with any better words to describe how this feels."

"Like it was meant to be?" I asked.

"Yeah. I guess knowing that I had Kar's blessing helped me with my feelings too."

Beck kissed me, first gently, then with more heat. When he reached down and grasped my growing cock, I knew it would be a while before we made it out of bed.

———

It turned out that we were both versatile, and I got to play the top role this morning. That led to a short nap, followed by blow jobs as we showered together, making it about ten thirty by the time we were dressed and heading out in search of breakfast. We went to Sam's and ate omelets with home fries and drank lots of coffee.

"Can you tell me a little bit about Tony?" Beck asked as we dined.

"What do you want to know?"

"I'm not really sure," he replied, "I guess I just …"

"Hey, you're not nervous, are you? Don't be. Tony may come across as a bit gruff until he gets to know you, but he's harmless."

"I'll try to calm down, but look, he's your friend, and I don't want him to think that I'm taking advantage of you due to my situation or anything."

"Relax, it'll be fine." I sipped my coffee, trying to figure out where to start. "I've known Tony for quite a few years now." I recounted Tony's background and how he had come to own the Raven's Claw.

"I met Tony because of the shop, really. I went in one day just to look around a bit, and we started chatting. Tony has a tiny touch of the gift—not so much that he can chat with spirits the way I can but enough that he can sense when someone else has the gift. He started referring folks to me if he thought I could help them, and that led to my officially starting up my business, if you will. Before that, I did a lot of odd jobs and worked as a stock boy, a dishwasher, things like that. Anything I could do to make ends meet. But Tony believed in me, and now I deal with the paranormal pretty much full-time."

"That's fascinating. I'll need to remember to thank Tony for helping you like that."

"Just don't lay it on too thick. He already has an overinflated opinion of himself." I grinned.

"Noted."

———

ONCE AGAIN, I stopped at the nearby café to get a cup of tea for Tony. I explained to Beck that I'd never dream of showing up at the shop empty-handed.

The bell over the door jingled as we entered, and Tony walked through the doorway from his office.

"Hey, Travis," he called out in greeting. He was dressed in

his usual attire: black jeans, black, long-sleeved T-shirt, and a leather cord around his neck with several amulets and crystals hanging from it.

"Hi, Tone," I replied. "I've brought a visitor with me. This"—I gestured—"is Beckett Gray. Beck, I'd like you to meet Tony Dawes." Tony accepted the takeout cup.

"Mr. Gray," Tony said, hand outstretched, "it's a pleasure to finally meet you. Travis has told me a little about you and your situation."

"Very nice to meet you as well, Mr. Dawes. And please, call me Beck."

"Then you must call me Tony. After all, if I'm not mistaken, Travis has become very fond of you, so we'll all be friends now, right? And of course, we're mutually acquainted with Valerie."

Beck's eyes scanned his surroundings. "This is a very interesting place you have here, Tony."

"Thank you. Feel free to look around. I'm happy to answer any questions you might have."

"I was thinking it might be a good idea to get Beck a crystal or two," I told Tony. "After all, everyone can use some protection, right?"

"That's actually a very good idea," Tony agreed. "Let's see what we can find."

We followed Tony to a counter along one side of the space, where a glass display case was filled with neatly arranged crystals.

"Tony, did I mention that Beck does some writing in his spare time? Maybe something to enhance creativity as well."

"Sure, give me a moment." Tony pulled out a black velvet pad and examined the stones in the case, choosing some after a few moments. An elaborate silver filigree cap was attached to each crystal to allow it to be hung from a chain or cord.

"Okay, I'd suggest these to start with. We can always add or modify the selection later if you want." Beck and I gazed down at the three stones Tony had selected. "This"—Tony pointed to the first stone—"is labradorite. You may recognize it since Travis wears one. It offers protection against negative energy and also helps spark the imagination. It's often called the stone of transformation. And I like that fact that you would both have one."

"This next one is apatite," Tony explained, picking up a blue stone that reminded me of the ocean. "It assists in creative problem-solving, stimulates the intellect, and enhances creativity. And finally, this one"—he touched a beautiful yellow stone—"is citrine. Citrine helps you get things done and fills you with inspiration and abundance." Tony looked at Beck and smiled. "I think the combination of these three will be really good for you."

"Okay," said Beck, a bit hesitantly.

"Beck, if you're not ready for this, that's okay. I just thought—"

"It's not that at all," Beck spoke over me. "I've actually been thinking of this since you mentioned it to me. A few months ago, I would have said it's all hogwash, but now, not so much." He turned to Tony. "How much will all this cost me?"

I spoke first. "Nothing. It's my gift to you."

"Actually," Tony chimed in, "I'll split the cost—the wholesale cost—with Travis. Think of it as a welcome-to-the-family gift from both of us. Let me grab a cord to put these on. Would you prefer leather or silk?"

"When you put it that way, how can I say no?" Beck

grinned, and I felt a flutter in my stomach. I was falling hard for this man. "As for the cord, leather, please. Thank you both for this."

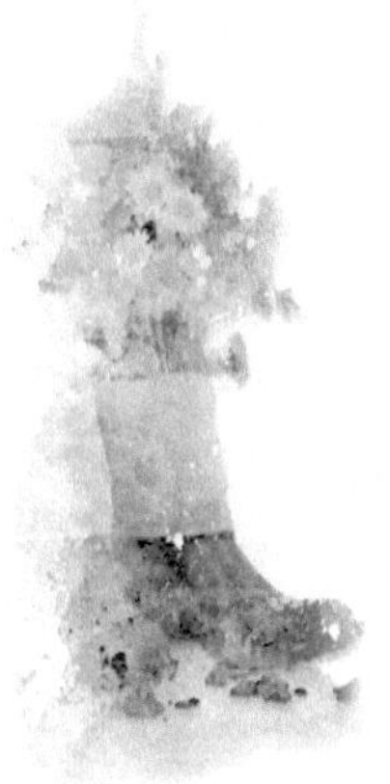

# thirty-one

BECK

HALLOWEEN WAS JUST a few days away, and I'd been getting more and more anxious as it neared. When I had last spoken to Kar, he'd said that he'd visit again before he moved on, but that was weeks ago, and I hadn't seen any sign of him since then. I was having a difficult time concentrating on work that afternoon; Val even pulled me aside at one point.

"What the hell's going on, Beck? You're clearly distracted. Talk to me."

I explained the situation and expressed my fears that somehow Kar would move on without contacting me again.

"Don't be ridiculous," she scoffed. "Kar was a man of his word. He wouldn't do that to you." Val was always the voice of reason. I was once again thankful to have her in my life.

"Thanks, sweetheart," I said affectionately. "My brain knows that, but my heart keeps second-guessing everything."

"Oh, honey." She patted my shoulder. "It's gonna be okay."

The end of the day couldn't come fast enough, then finally, Val and I arrived at Fiddler's in record time. Travis was already there when we arrived; he'd started joining in for our weekly unwinds a couple of weeks earlier. We settled in at the bar, got our preferred beverages, and shared food and light conversation for a few hours.

Travis followed me home to spend the night. We were at a point in our relationship where we still wanted our own spaces most of the time but managed to arrange sleepovers a couple of times a week, most often on the weekends. We entered the house via the back door, and as soon as Travis stepped over the threshold, he stopped, a look of surprise on his face.

"What's wrong?"

"Pretty sure Kar's here," he said quietly. He walked quickly to the den.

"Kar, is that you?" he called out. Then to me, "Yep, he's here. He says we should sit down; he wants to talk to us."

"Hi, Kar," I said quietly. While I fully believed that he was with us, for some reason I still felt a little uncomfortable actually speaking with my deceased husband.

Travis relayed Kar's message to me. "He says that even though he's been away, he's managed to keep an eye on us, and we seem happy together. It means a lot to him."

"You're going to move on, aren't you, sweetheart?" I asked.

"Yes. It's time, Toddy. Now that I know you're happy, I can head east and see what's next for me."

"East? Why east?" I couldn't hide the confusion in my voice.

"Honestly, I don't really know. It's just that when I feel the pull to move on, I get the urge to head east. Joseph says it's like that for everyone."

"Who's Joseph?"

"Another spirit I met wandering around here. He's become a good friend and taught me so much about this place. Joseph has been here longer than I have. He's still not ready to move on but hopefully soon. I want him to be happy."

"When do you think you'll move on?" Travis asked as himself.

"Soon. Most likely on Samhain. Joseph says a lot of spirits go at that time."

"Does that mean you won't visit again?" I choked out. "I'm not sure I'm ready, Kar."

"You are, my dear. You have Travis; I can see the affection between the two of you. This is your chance for more happiness in your life. Grab onto it with both hands and know that I will love you forever."

"I do have feelings for Travis, but part of my heart will always be yours, Kar."

"I know, sweetheart. Be well. Remember, I'll always love you. Travis, thank you for taking care of him."

Travis was quiet for a few moments, then his focus changed. While we were conversing with Kar, he'd been staring toward my desk, I assumed because Kar was standing there. Now his gaze shifted, searching the room for something. Finally, he looked at me.

"He's gone," he whispered.

A sob escaped my lips. "This feels surreal. A part of me feels selfish. I don't want him to go. I know, that's weird coming from someone who didn't believe all that long ago. But I want him to be happy too. And if moving on is what he needs to do, then I'm okay with that even if it means I won't have any more contact with him."

"Tell me what I can do to help you, Beck."

"Hold me. Take me to bed and just hold me, please."

———

WE SPENT a quiet day at home on Saturday. I was still feeling a bit unsettled and wasn't in the mood to be out among people. Travis was understanding, telling me Auntie Mae had given him a book that she thought might be of interest to him, so he went out to his car to get it and sat with it on the sofa in the den.

I ordered some groceries online and then read for a while, trying to escape into the pages of my current book. When Val texted me, asking if we were doing game night, I bit the bullet and said yes, thinking I'd wallowed long enough.

"Any thoughts on what we could do for dinner tonight?" I asked Travis.

"Well, if you'd like, I could make some of Grandma's potato salad, and we could have that with burgers."

"That's a great idea!" I exclaimed. "I've actually dreamt of Grandma's potato salad."

Just then, the doorbell rang, announcing the delivery of the groceries I'd ordered.

"Perfect timing," Travis said. "I'll help you put everything away, and I can make sure you've got all the ingredients. If not, I can run out and pick things up."

Fortunately, I had everything Travis needed. He set to work in my kitchen so that the salad would have time to chill for a while to let the flavors marry. Before I knew it, Val arrived, and we began a pleasant evening together.

"Oh my God," Val effused when she tasted Grandma's specialty. "This is so good!"

Later, we played a game of Mexican Train, and the very competitive Val won, which was often the case. When Val left, Travis and I went up to bed, where he made slow, passionate love to me. It was exactly what I needed.

———

IT WAS HALLOWEEN, and I was feeling both sad and excited. Sad because Kar was planning on crossing over to the next plane tonight, and that meant I'd never hear from him again. But excited for him, knowing he'd finally be at peace.

Val knew I wasn't really myself, so she relegated me to the small space we called my office—a closet-like area without a door—to do paperwork while she managed the staff, filled prescriptions, and spoke with customers. When five o'clock finally rolled around, she scooted me out the door, handing me a bag of candy for the trick-or-treaters.

Knowing I didn't want to be alone, I'd asked Travis to come over for dinner and to spend the night. He was waiting in my driveway when I pulled in. Hmmm, maybe I should just give him the extra key I'd had made.

We ordered pizza and took turns answering the door to hand out bars of chocolate, keeping conversation to a minimum. I'm sure Travis understood my mood, but his presence soothed me in a way I couldn't really describe. I don't think I would have survived the night without him.

Once the little—and not-so-little—visitors ceased, I turned off the light on the front porch and brought our empty glasses into the kitchen. I saw a few small sprigs of wildflowers sitting in the center of the island.

"Travis." My breath caught in my throat. "Can you come here, please?"

He hurried in. "What's wrong?"

I pointed to the island, my finger trembling slightly. "You didn't put those there by any chance, did you?"

"No," he said softly. "It must have been ..."

"Kar," we said simultaneously.

"Goodbye, sweetheart," I whispered. "Safe journey. I love you."

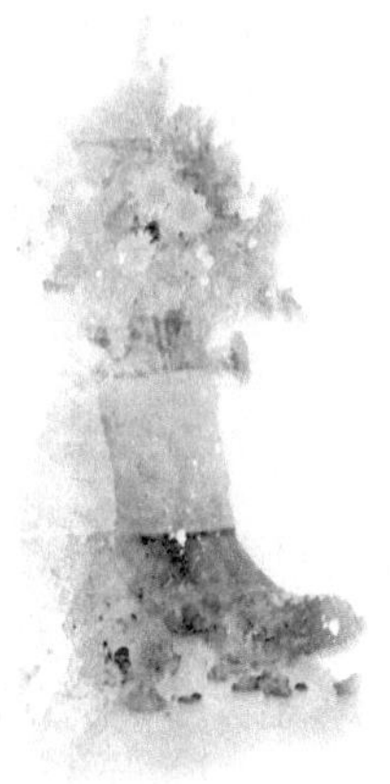

# epilogue

*Six months later*

BECK

I woke wrapped in Travis, his arms encircling my chest and belly. No doubt about it, the man loved to cuddle in bed. I reached for my phone, checking the day's weather—warm and sunny for the first of May. I'd been thinking about it for a while and knew exactly what I wanted to do today.

I slowly extracted myself from the arms surrounding me and padded to the bathroom. After relieving myself, I climbed into the shower and was washing my hair when the shower door opened, and a very naked Travis stepped in.

"Mind if I join you?" he asked.

"Not at all." I smiled.

We washed each other, which led to a blow job or two, then

dried off and dressed in relative silence. Being together with Travis had proven to be a balm for my soul. We fit together so well and didn't need to fill empty spaces with endless chatter.

"Any plans for today?" he finally asked as we descended the stairs.

"Actually, yes," I said, prepping the coffee maker for our much-needed caffeine. "As long as you don't think it's too weird."

"Sweetheart," he said, kissing the back of my neck, "I love you. Even if it is weird, I'll go along with it. After all, it was weirdness that brought us together, right?" Yeah, he loved me. We'd both said those magic words to each other a couple of months ago. For what it's worth, Travis said them first.

"Since it's Beltane, I was thinking I might like to go to the cemetery to visit Kar's grave. I know he's not actually there, but it just feels right. Perhaps leave some flowers on his grave. I dunno, maybe it's silly, but I've been thinking about that a lot lately."

"I don't think it's silly at all. He crossed over six months ago. I think this is the perfect way to honor him." Travis paused as if unsure how to proceed. He sipped at the coffee I'd poured for him and finally looked at me. "I can hang out here while you go or maybe meet you somewhere after."

"No, silly." I kissed him lightly on the lips. "You're coming with me. I'm gonna pick some wildflowers from the side garden to put on the grave. After that, we'll go to breakfast."

"If you're sure ..." he started.

"Of course, I'm sure. You're just as much a part of this as Kar and me."

———

"That was nice," Travis said after we were seated at Sam's. "It's a beautiful spot to sit and be still." The cemetery where Kar's body rested had lots of small park-like spaces with benches and trees. I didn't go there very often, but I always felt better for having visited.

"Before I forget, when's your next appointment with Dr. Chandler? I wanted to put it in my calendar." We'd discussed Travis's issues with alcohol a few months earlier, and he'd begun seeing a therapist.

"Tuesday at four. Maybe we could meet for dinner after?"

"Why don't you just come to the house? That reminds me, there's something else I've been meaning to ask you," I stated.

"Of course." Travis looked at me expectantly.

"We've been spending more and more time together," I said. The reality was that we'd seamlessly divided our time between his house and mine, rarely spending an evening without the other. "Maybe it's time for us to move in together." I looked into his eyes, waiting for a reaction.

"It's funny that you mention that." Travis smiled. "I've been thinking about the same thing. I don't think either one of us wants to sell our respective homes, but I had an idea about that."

"Oh, good, because that was one of the things that was troubling me about this."

"My thought is that I could move in with you since your house is bigger and frankly, nicer than mine."

I started to protest, but Travis shushed me. Yes, my house was larger, but I loved the coziness of his place too.

"And while I don't want to sell Grandma's house, I could rent it out. It's in a nice neighborhood, and that way it stays in the family."

"I love that idea!" I said excitedly. "How soon do you think we could make this happen?"

"Well, if you don't have anything else planned for today, we could pack up a few of my things and bring them home. Once we've got the stuff I want, I'll make the arrangements to have the place cleaned and rented. I'm sure Tony knows people who could help with that."

Later that day as I helped Travis unpack the final box of his belongings, I thought about Kar and how there was no doubt that just as he'd left muddy footprints on the front porch, he had also left footprints on my heart. Yes, I'd always love him, but I had learned that my heart was big enough that I could love another man too.

Travis was not just my friend and lover, he was now my home, and we would continue to build on this life we had started together.

Home. I liked the sound of that.

THE *End*

*Curious about Kar's friend Joseph?*
*Keep reading for a bonus chapter about him and what happens after Kar moves on.*

# bonus chapter

**Joseph**

I sat on the bench near the edge of the park, thinking about my life—and my death. I'd been wandering around here in this interim plane for about twelve years. Quite a long time. Most folks pass quickly to the next plane although a few linger here for a bit. But I hadn't met anyone who'd been here as long as I had.

The closest I'd come was my friend Karson. Yes, I thought I could call Kar my friend even though I only met him after we'd both passed on. Kar wandered the interim plane for five years, and I knew him for most of that time. But I've gotten ahead of myself. Let me back up a bit.

As I said, I passed on about twelve years ago, leaving my one true love alone in the world of the living. I was several years older than them and had experienced a few different health issues over the years, so I guess it wasn't surprising that I died first. I went peacefully in my sleep, but part of me wasn't really ready to go just then. So I lingered here in this place, wondering what to do next.

Many folks feel the need to pass through quickly, but I wanted to wait. I wanted to check in on my love, make sure they were okay. So I ignored the pull to head east, moving on to the next plane of existence, whatever that may be. Yes, I stayed. And stayed some more. Years passed, and still I stayed.

At one point early on, I decided that I was hanging around until my sweetheart was ready to join me. Something just felt wrong about moving on without them. Truth be told, the years passed fairly quickly. I'd spend lots of my time just watching them, making sure everything was okay. They still lived in the home we'd shared for thirty years, and it felt good to hang out at the old place even if they didn't know I was there.

I also spent a lot of time reading, visiting various libraries at night since I no longer needed to sleep. And I'd travel, too, revisiting places we'd been together over the years. Of course, I'd met lots of spirits—some moving on quickly but quite a few who lingered for a year or two. We'd talk about all manner of things, but I never spoke of my love. I kept that story close to my heart. Well, until I met Kar.

Karson Raycroft was an interesting man. Lingering in the interim plane to help his still-living husband find a new love. I thought that was quite admirable. Not that it was something I could have done. Anyway, I enjoyed the time I spent with Kar. I taught him how things worked here and to some degree helped him in his mission.

At first, I didn't share my story with Kar, but when his task was finished and he was ready to pass over to the next plane, I told him my whole story. We sat on this very bench one day, and I said I was waiting for the love of my life to join me so we could move on together.

"I got the sense that you were waiting for something to happen," Kar told me when I finished my tale. "I wasn't sure exactly what, but there was some kind of anticipation in your attitude."

"Well, it won't be long now," I said. "Their health has been failing, and they've been in a nursing home for the past couple of years. Don't ask me how I know, but I think they'll be joining me in the next few weeks."

Kar wished me well and said he was paying one last visit to his husband, Beck, and the new man in his life—a medium who had helped Beck understand what was happening with Kar. Then Kar would move on. That was about a week ago, and I must admit, I miss spending time with Kar. But it won't be long now.

———

Several days passed. I was meandering around our old neighborhood when I suddenly got the urge to go to the Meadow Glen Nursing Home. That's where they had been for the past couple of years. I willed myself there and stood in the corner of their room. Yes, it was almost time.

But I soon realized I didn't want to be in that room when it actually happened. I couldn't explain it, but I didn't want to see my love pass to this plane. I hurried outside and sat on one of the benches near the small pond next to the building, watching the ducks splash about. Here I'd sit until it happened.

Perhaps a few hours passed—time was a difficult concept here—but daylight was fading now, so I guessed at the interval. I turned to look at the front of the building, and I saw Anthony—*my Anthony!*—walking toward me. He no longer looked old and feeble; the cancer that had torn through his body had miraculously been erased. He looked like I remembered him from just before I passed.

"Joseph!" he called to me. "You're here."

"Of course I am, my love. Where else would I be?"

"You waited for me? All this time?"

"It seemed but a moment in the whole scheme of things. How could I go on without you?"

We embraced. We kissed. I felt whole again.

We sat together on the bench, hand in hand, and talked for hours, maybe days. I told him everything that I'd been up to while I waited. I spoke of Karson and his husband, Beckett, and Beck's new love, Travis.

"You did a wonderful thing helping Kar," Anthony told me.

"I hope so. And it helped pass the time while I waited for you."

"What happens now?"

"Now we move on together. To see what the next plane has in store for us."

And so we stood, held hands, and walked to the east. Together again for all eternity.

# a letter from rj

Dear Reader,

Thank you so much for reading Footprints on My Heart.

I'm hard at work on writing the next book. It will involved whichever characters are chattering away in my head at the moment.

Be sure to follow me on Amazon to be notified of new releases, and look for me on Facebook for sneak peeks of upcoming stories.

Please take a moment to write a review of Footprints on My Heart on Amazon and/or Goodreads. Reviews can make all the difference in helping a book show up in Amazon searches.

To to sign up for my newsletter, stop by rj-peterson.ck.page.

We have a great reader group on Facebook that can be found here: www.facebook.com/groups/rjpetersonsadventurers/

Finally, several of my titles are available on audio, narrated by the amazing Kevin Earlywine or the fabulous Cole Kurtz. They can be found here: link.rjpeterson.net/audio

Happy reading!

RJ

*P.S. Keep going for a free download!*

# free short story

**Download a copy of His Elevator Pitch**

Inspired by a writing prompt, His Elevator Pitch is the story of River, an unemployed executive assistant, and Thom, the department head of a prestigious multi-faceted corporation.

When a power failure takes out several city blocks in Boston, MA, they find themselves stuck in an elevator with nothing but time on their hands.

Conversation ensues and when power is restored, River goes off to his interview, thinking that's the end of his encounter with the handsome stranger. Or is it?

———

This story features many of the themes my writing is known for: older guys, sweet-with-heat encounters, low or no angst, and always a happily ever after.

SCAN THE CODE TO DOWNLOAD

# about the author

Hi, I'm RJ! I'm a retired graphic designer. An avid reader—preferably while sipping a vodka martini or bourbon on the rocks—I've had a long and varied career, including library page, car wash attendant, travel agent, and graphic designer in the marijuana industry. In addition, I worked in the banking industry for twenty-five years. I love to travel and have been on 65+ cruises. When not on a cruise, my husband & I live in New England.

I never planned to be a writer, but a fateful day in January, 2021 changed it all. I woke with a story stuck in my head and started typing. The more I type, the more story ideas I get.

**Find all my links here:**

# want to read more?

**The New Adventures in Love**

Love On The Horizon

Love For The Holidays

Love On The Potomac

Love In The Mediterranean

Love Is For Family

*(Coming in 2025)*

———

**Hawthorne Bluff**

Finding Finlay

Addicted to Ashton

Chasing Courtland

*(Coming in 2026)*

———

**SEAsons of Love**

Love at Frost Sight

Resting Grinch Face

Don't Claus a Scene

Great Chemis-Tree

———

———

**All my book links in one place!**